Menage's Way:

Triple Crown Collection

Menage's Way:

Triple Crown Collection

Victor L. Martin

www.urbanbooks.net

Urban Books, LLC
97 N18th Street
Wyandanch, NY 11798

Menage's Way: Triple Crown Collection

ISBN 13: 978-1-62286-740-0
ISBN 10: 1-62286-740-8

First Urban Books Mass Market Printing November 2016
First Trade Paperback Printing (November 2004)
Printed in the United States of America

10 9 8 7 6 5 4 3 2 1

Distributed by Kensington Publishing Corp.
Submit Orders to:
Customer Service
400 Hahn Road
Westminster, MD 21157-4627
Phone: 1-800-733-3000
Fax: 1-800-659-2436

Dedications

Sandra J. Martin—Mom Angie R. Martin—Sis
Dominique A. Covington—Nephew Janayia
A. Martin . . . B.K.A. Jizzy—Niece Tremika M.
Smith—Sis

I love you deeply. REVELATION 2:10

Acknowledgments

Again I must give up the most thanks to my friend and typist, Kim A. Carroll. Let's keep the books rolling. To all of my readers that gave me praise on my first work of fiction, I'll stay humble and I'll stay true. Thank you deeply for your support.

Tyreka D. Batts, forgive a nigga as I forgive you. Jennifer Ray, thanks for being a friend since the fourth grade. Write me tonight. To everyone in Johnston County, God's will, my next book will be set in Selma, think it's a game? Another big one goes out to Tammy, thank you for your words that kept me going. You're the best office manager I know. TCP is on top. Jason Poole, hold it strong, this storm won't last forever. I'm going on two years in this single man cell and I refuse to be broken! Don't pity me, just understand.

Keama T. Eason, thank you for showing me the true meaning of the word friend and thanks for understanding me. Bonnie, I'll always owe you one. And much love to the H-Q-I-C (Head Queen in Charge) Vickie Stringer. Mere words won't reach the love and thanks that I hold for you. And to my editor, thank you.

Prologue

Felix sat back and folded his hands. "They want it to go down at ten but he-or they-will call again at nine thirty. We'll know how to find them . . . and hopefully Chandra as well at seven. Menage, it will be up to you on how we move on this, but my offer still stands to make the trade."

Menage stood and looked at Felix then Covington. "Just call me when you get the location," he said turning to leave the boat. Felix got up from his seat, but he knew it was pointless to call after him. He could see the pain that Menage tried to hide.

"Take care of him," he said turning to Dough-Low.

Dough-Low shrugged his massive shoulders. "He's a grown-ass man," he replied before turning to follow Menage.

***

"So what's the plan?" yelled Dough-Low over the roar of the speedboat engine.

"We just wait . . . time will tell."

Chapter 1

Just Doin' The Damn Thang!

"You gonna try to take her back by force, ain't cha?" Dough-Low said as he tugged on his seat strap.

"Don't know."

"Well, I'm wit' ya all the way, dog. Fuck it. Whateva, whateva!"

Menage headed back toward Miami, reaching a speed of up to 175 miles per hour. When they reached Miami, he left Vapor on the speedboat and rode with Dough-Low in his Yukon Denali XL as they made up their minds to hit the strip on bikes.

At Felix's place, Menage mounted a 1300-R Suzuki Hayabusa and Dough-Low picked out a silver and black new generation Yamaha YZF-R1. Dough-Low sat on the R1 with his helmet visor up as he revved up the engine. "Yo, son, I'ma show ya how ta ride like the Double R," he yelled. Menage glanced back at him, knowing Dough-Low was trying to get him to smile and ease up. It was working.

"Don't underestimate me, Dough," he said as he turned back the throttle, revving up the bike's engine. Dough-Low flipped down the tinted visor and leaned his weight forward over the fuel tank. He gunned the engine on the YZF-R1 and let the clutch go with both feet dragging on the side. The bike's front end was about to rise, but Dough-Low held it down as it vanished in thick smoke, shooting forward with a whine. Seconds later, Menage did the same on his powerful Suzuki.

Spring break was in full swing on the South Beach strip. Menage and Dough-Low sat on their bikes watching all the action. Dough-Low was looking at all the niggas he could catch slipping, but today they were lucky; he wasn't in jack mode and he moved his attention to the thong contest across the street. All heads turned when a black Dodge Ram SRT-10 appeared. It was packed with girls dancing and stripping in the back as Too Short's "Shake That Monkey" blared from its system. It was a sight to see as it slowly cruised down the street. "Damn!" was all Dough-Low could say as a dark-skinned girl tossed him her thong. Menage looked, but he showed no emotion whatsoever. For him everything seemed to move in slow motion with no sound. Girls in high heels and thongs walked by, touching his bike and asking his name, but it was as if they weren't there. Smacking their lips, they moved on. Even cars and SUVs with booming systems, turning corners on three wheels didn't grab his attention. Sweat ran down Menage's face and he ignored it and everything around him as he closed his eyes and thought of his girl. Nothing else mattered but her safe return. *Fuck the chop shop, the money and the dream.* All he wanted was Chandra. He thought about breaking rule number one-no speedballin', but he knew it would cost him his life as well as Chandra's if he rushed in with some lame ass plan . . . if and when he found out where she was being held. He opened his eyes to clear his head. Something had to give.

Across the street, two girls were up on a stage rubbing their bare breasts together. The crowd went wild as they began to French kiss. Menage reached for his helmet.

"You ready to go?" Dough-Low asked. Menage nodded and started up his bike. He didn't know where he was going but he felt the need to just be on the move. Today it all had to go down and it scared the hell out of him.

***

"Yo, Dough, we got to come up with a plan," Menage said. He and Dough-Low were sitting on their bikes watching a quick, pick-up basketball game at Liberty Square Park on Martin Luther King Boulevard on Sixty-second Street in Liberty City.

"I know, but it all depends on where dem cats gonna be at plus we have ta wait till seven, right?" Dough-Low said glancing at the sky, thinking of the satellite somewhere above them.

"Yeah," Menage said looking at his watch. It was almost four thirty now.

"Don't worry, yo. We gonna hold it down. Don't even stress it!" Dough-Low wondered how Menage would act when the pressure came down. He knew Menage had something that he didn't—a conscience.

"Menage, is that you?"

Both men turned at the sound of the female voice. Coming up the sidewalk was Irish and some other girl. Irish was only eighteen, dark-skinned, five feet eight inches and 150 pounds. She wasn't fat just thick, and the slightly shorter girl standing next to her could've passed for her twin. They both wore DKNY bodysuits. "Hey, boo," purred Irish as she walked up to Menage and hugged him. Dough-Low watched the silky material grip her ass like a second skin. "You forgot my number or somethin'? What's really goin' on, nigga?"

Menage closed his eyes, wishing he didn't have to be bothered with her. Now just wasn't the time. Irish was only good for sex and just fucking around. "I been out of town. What's up?"

"Boy, please. I seen your ass at the Limelight all up on that girl. I would've said somethin', but I was wit' my baby daddy," she said smiling. "Who dat?" she said directing her chin toward Dough-Low.

"My man, Dough-Low . . . Dough, dis Irish."

"Oh, that's all I am, boy? Nah, I'm just trippin'. It's all good, though. I know you be out doin' your thing-thing, but you still could've called me. It's been . . . uh . . . two weeks, boy!"

Before Menage could try to explain, a blue Chevy '64 convertible pulled up carrying three wild-looking men wearing dreads. The girl standing next to Irish had the look of fear on her face. The Chevy came to a stop.

"Yo, what da fuck wrong wit' you, Passion!" yelled the driver. "Bring your hot ass over here. 'Round here fuckin' wit' these herb-ass niggas!" He and the man in the passenger's seat got out, but the one in the back remained in the vehicle. Menage looked at Dough-Low and then back at the two men.

"She ain't out here talkin' to nobody, nigga, you trippin'!" Irish said with her hands on her hips.

"Bitch, shut da fuck up!" the driver said giving Irish the screw face. "Now, which one of you lames tryin' to spit at my shorty?" Passion lowered her head and said nothing. "Oh, y'all can't speak English!"

"First off, dog, who the hell you beefin' at?" Dough-Low said as he got off his bike.

"Oh, so you wanna be a brave-ass nigga, huh?"

"Pretty much!" Dough-Low said.

"So what's up, nigga?" the driver said with his arms spread wide.

"Don't talk me to death."

Menage's adrenalin started to flow as he watched the guy still seated in the back of the Chevy. "What the hell y'all gonna fight for? Damn, J-Money, you stupid as hell. l swear!" Irish said slowly taking a step back. She was no fool. Nothing moved in slow motion for Menage any longer when J-Money pulled a pistol on Dough-Low.

Chandra was alive, but far from well on the boat with the mercenaries. When she tried to explain to Scorpion that she wasn't Felix's girl, he snapped and slapped her across the face so hard that it left a small cut under her eye. That was the last time she said anything about the mix-up. She sat on the corner of the bed looking at the floor in a daze. She knew she had to stay alive no matter what they did to her. Menage would come for her once he knew of her whereabouts, and he would do anything for she and their unborn child.

Chandra didn't hear Myrmidon and Scorpion walk into the cabin. She cringed when she felt Scorpion's touch on the back of her neck. "Now, is that any way to treat me when I'm keeping you alive?" Scorpion said as he yanked her hair, snapping her neck back. She held back her scream as the pain danced in the roots of her scalp. "I don't care if you are Felix's bitch or not. I'm going to get what I want!" he said. He caught Myrmidon standing in the doorway looking at Chandra's exposed legs. "Maybe we can have a little fun with her. I can tell she'll like it. If not . . . well, I guess we'll just have to see what she'll do. But since it'll be her last fuck, she just might not put up too much of a fight."

"I'm having a baby," Chandra said hoping they would at least think of her child.

"Like I give a fuck. They say it's good to kill two birds with one stone. Ain't that right,

Myrmidon?" Myrmidon only nodded and hoped that Scorpion couldn't read the mixed feelings he felt inside. Killing was his job, but rape . . . that wasn't in his book. Myrmidon still thought of himself as a soldier with a code. But he knew he couldn't stop Scorpion if he tried to rape her. He needed to get paid and the woman before him wasn't worth a dime to him. He would make some excuse to leave when Scorpion made his move on her. The best he could and would do was order his men not to join in on the act. Scorpion wasn't a soldier in Myrmidon's book; he was more of a power-crazed government spook. Myrmidon licked his dry lips as Scorpion forced the girl on her back. She was strong, but Myrmidon saw the tears falling down her face. He knew she was about to break. He could easily put a bullet in the back of Scorpion's skull . . . to hell with the money.

Myrmidon gripped his pistol. Scorpion had his fingers between Chandra's legs, amazed that she wasn't putting up a fight. Just as Scorpion stood up to take off his pants, one of the mercenaries banged on the door. Scorpion turned around and Myrmidon lowered his pistol and let the man into the room. "What the hell is it?" Scorpion yelled before Myrmidon had a chance to speak.

"We got a large contact on the radar screen. As of now it's just doing a race track pattern, but when we moved it seemed to have . . . like followed us." Scorpion fixed his clothes and made his way past Myrmidon. Making sure Scorpion was gone, Myrmidon reached in his pocket and pulled out a packet of ointment. He gave it to Chandra and left the cabin, locking the door behind him.

Scorpion looked at the glowing red dot on the small radar screen. He began typing commands on the Old Russian hardware.

"What is it?" Myrmidon asked standing behind him, peering over his shoulder.

"Just a second . . . what we have here is a U.S. Navy guided missile frigate . . . either the USS Reuben James or Samuel B. Roberts on an exercise."

"Let's hope so," Myrmidon said, not afraid to show his concern for the sudden appearance of the ship.

"Relax," Scorpion said. "If it was after us, we'd be long gone. Anyway, this game is over tonight. We'll call Felix and inform him that his girl is at the airfield in Homestead . . . where you'll be waiting," he added looking at Myrmidon. "We'll allow him to talk to her over the phone while two of your men fly with me to the island. It's up to you to take out Felix at the airport. You two stay on the boat until it all goes down," he said pointing at two of the mercenaries. "Once I make the pick-up, I'll call and you'll all know the escape plan."

"What do we do with the girl when it all goes down?"asked one of the mercenaries who'd be staying on the boat.

"Kill her! Timing is important, men," said Scorpion looking at his watch. "Let's lock and load. I got a big surprise for our friend, Felix."

Dough-Low stood up on the cockpit of Menage's speedboat, reenacting the fight he had and won at Liberty Square Park. "Yo, it's true! I scooped that fool and boom! Clown gonna pull a burner on me that jammed!" Dough-Low had beaten the man until he was unconscious. Then he pistol-whipped him with his own broken gun. Menage had the shakes since he had to draw down on the kid who stayed in the car after carefully walking up and finding an SKS rifle between his legs. It was almost five now, and he looked down at his medallion and glanced at the chipped *D* that was struck in the hit. He ignored the sweat running down his back and the holster holding the two Glock-9s under his arms. Nothing mattered anymore. All he wanted was his girl, and he was unconcerned about any bullshit he had to go through to get her back. His mind was made up. He'd give his life for her safe return.

The CIA satellite finally slowed down on its high-speed trip from the Middle East. It was programmed to snap ten shots of the area where the signal came from, capturing Scorpion's conversation with Felix on tape. When it came to a stop, its high-powered camera lens zoomed in on a boat with five men loading a box onto a smaller boat tied next to it. The CIA wanted Scorpion out of the picture at all costs.

USS Reuben James (FFG-57)

Stanley Walters was seasick again. The CIA field officer was rushed to the frigate only two hours earlier by an SH-60F helicopter from Miami. The ride was quick but unpleasant; the dare devil pilot had skimmed over the sea close to 120 knots only seventy-five feet above the water. Standing next to him was the ship's commander, Lieutenant Commander Otis Atkins. His black skin seemed to shine in the sun's glare.

"Sir, may I use your phone to call Washington?" asked Walters, wishing he could get the heck off the boat. The smile on Atkins' face quickly faded.

"Son, you're CIA. Sure you can use a phone. Matter of fact, I'll have a Marine escort you to my personal phone in my office."

Atkins didn't like that his ship was called back from heading on a nice long trip to Spain. He knew it was bad news when the powers that be told him to welcome the spooky CIA Agent aboard. He knew well enough not to ask any questions, but it had to be big for the U.S. Navy to change his orders. Nothing major was on CNN and everyone wanted to know what the hell was going on. He knew one thing: it wasn't an exercise.

The U.S. Marine military police closed Atkins' door, leaving Agent Walters alone. He sat on the edge of the large desk and placed his call to D.C. Seconds later, the Director of Central Intelligence, Joe Troublefield, answered the phone. "Do you have a visual yet?" he asked quickly.

Stanley loosened his tie. "No, sir. We're waiting for the bird to get into position now." He looked at his watch. "Has the KGB released any pictures of our man?"

"No."

Stanley rolled his eyes. *Mission impossible,* he thought. "So how are we gonna get the go to loose a missile on him if we don't know if he's there or not?"

"I thought the same thing, but it's his voice. We have a one hundred percent match, and this can get real messy if we let him slip away. And about the girl . . . it's more important that we take Scorpion out-quick and fast."

Stanley knew about the girl Scorpion was holding and he wasn't fond of taking her life just to take care of him. As soon as he was brought in on the case, he asked for the F.B.I. to send in the Hostage Rescue Team but his idea was shot down. He called Troublefield with the hopes that he would change his mind about a senseless missile launch but his mind was made up. Making sure Troublefield had hung up first, Stanley slammed the phone down on its hook and stormed out of the office, making his way back to the bridge as the ship maintained its steady pace.

"Well, well, well, I must say our government is up to something on this fine day," said the computer whiz who also operated Felix's radar post on his island.

"What is it?" asked his assistant as he stood up to look over his shoulder at the computer screen.

"If I'm correct, I think it's a CIA recon bird, whatever the hell that is. It got here fast and it's not supposed to be in this area. I'm going to break into its relay and frequency and see if I can see what it beams back down to good ol' earth. If I can do that, we'll have a head start on the trace, but once I tap in, whomever the bird belongs to will know that I'm online and that's not good," he said as his fingers combed over the keyboard.

"Can you do it?"

"Can a bird fly?"

"Dude, all birds can't fly . . . well, most can!"

The two remaining mercenaries stood on the rocking speedboat as Scorpion and their leader, Myrmidon, along with their fellow mercenaries headed to Miami on the smaller boat. Down below on the speedboat, Chandra was no longer tied to the bed.

"Think we'll have enough time to do her?" asked the blond mercenary moments later.

"Sure, but I go first." They both rushed down to the deck below as soon as Scorpion's boat was out of sight.

***
6:12pm-Aboard Felix's Yacht

"Yes, I got it," yelled the computer whiz. "Gimme a pen so I can jot down the position, dude. And hurry up before I have to terminate the signal!" He glanced at the screen as the position of the call appeared. He was able to download two of the ten pictures the CIA recon satellite took before the break-in was discovered. He was shocked when he realized the call was traced only forty miles from the yacht.

"Call Menage and pass the info on to him," Felix said as he walked to his bar. He was now back on the island and out on his landing pad. Two trucks held his coke. "I don't like this at all," he said to one of his bodyguards. Felix was glad they now had the jump on Scorpion, but it was all up to Menage on what their next move would be.

6:13pm-Aboard Menage's Way

Menage rushed below the deck to pull out a map to find the spot where Felix said the call was traced to. Dough-Low looked over his shoulder as he loaded the weapons. Menage didn't know if the boat holding Chandra would be there or not, and he knew he couldn't ride up on them because they still had her.

"So what do we do, son?" Dough-Low asked.

Menage tore the map in half and balled it up. He looked at his watch. "Yo, let's just get as close as we can without us drawing attention and then . . . man, fuck . . . this is bullshit!"

Dough-Low placed a hand on his friend's shoulder. "Look, dog, let's just wait till they call. Right now the ball is in our court, so just chill, son, 'cause we gonna get your girl back. Oh, it's true!"

Aboard USS Reuben James, CIA Field Officer Stanley Walters sat in the quiet Command Information Center with Lieutenant Commander Otis Atkins.

"So what's the story?" asked Atkins glancing at Walters, hoping he would be leaving soon and off his ship. Walters cleared his throat. He was glad that the motion sickness patch was working. He quickly told the lieutenant about the pictures and the voice match.

"So is it your man or not? And since I haven't been cleared to what is fully going on, I do wish to know how I will be of help. This is my ship. My baby, my life, so please, Walters, don't pull my leg on this one."

Walters knew he wasn't 100 percent sure that Scorpion was there, but Troublefield was breathing fire up his ass and they wanted action and a body. "I have direct orders from our Commander in Chief, the President of the United States, to use a missile to take out that boat. That's as simple as I can put it, sir," he said.

Atkins looked at him in disbelief. "Son, I do hope you know what you're asking me to do. And since we're not in peace time, I do hope this is for a major reason," he said looking Walters directly in the eye. He then stood up and gave the order to sound general quarters. The fire control gunner already had a lock on the small boat. No one knew who was on it or why it had to be destroyed. Sailors ran to their stations as the Reuben James slowed to ten knots. Atkins knew whoever was on that boat wouldn't even know what hit them; they had no radar. The cruise missile was programmed to hit the stationary target, providing it didn't move, but if it did, the missile would not arm itself and would then fall harmlessly into the ocean. "Ready on tube two, sir," said the Weapons Officer.

"Fire . . . two," said Atkins. "God help us all." The cruise missile shot out of the long gray tube in a slight arch fully engulfed in smoke. When it was at a safe distance from the ship, its rocket motor engaged. It quickly picked up speed, leaving a puff of smoke as it dropped twenty feet above the water. Its top speed was five hundred knots. Once it reached the target, the proximity fuse would set the missile off from fifty yards in a deadly explosion. The entire crew had their eyes on the two dots—one blue and one red. Once the red was within fifty yards, both dots would vanish.

"What's the ETA?" asked Atkins as he slowly sat down.

"One minute and five seconds and counting sir!"

"Good. Ready . . . ASAR, ASAP," Atkins said, knowing that there would be nothing left of the boat, but those were the rules. Seconds later, the search rescue helicopter prepared for takeoff.

Aboard the Mercenaries' Boat

"Fuck! Tie the bitch's legs up, man, before she kicks me again," said the blond mercenary as he ripped off Chandra's shirt. He then slapped her with the palm of his hand. "Yeah, bitch!" he said as he started to pump himself to hardness. "You're gonna like this."

"Come on, dude, don't take forever!" yelled his partner, who had just finished prying Chandra's legs apart and securely tying them with rope to the bedposts. The blond mercenary felt that Chandra was dry and he slapped her again, spitting in her face this time. He looked to see if his partner was watching the show, but he wasn't there. Chandra's hands were again tied above her head and the blond mercenary smiled and licked her breasts. He was on fire. Supporting his upper body with the palms of his hands, he rammed his penis deep inside of her, but she didn't move or cry out. "Say you like, yes . . . say . . ." All of a sudden he was thrown off the bed as the boat jerked forward and turned sharply. He rolled to his knees and stood back up to put on his pants. "What the fuck are you doing up there?" he yelled, falling again as the boat turned sharply once more.

"Missile coming in, you better—" His partner never got to finish his statement.

"Let's move!" Scorpion yelled at the two mercenaries. They had just dropped off Myrmidon with his sniper rifle at the old airfield in Homestead. Scorpion strapped himself in the seat of the small but capable Augusta 109 helicopter. He was planning to pay Felix's island a visit ahead of time. "You guys be ready and keep a look out for any other air traffic," he yelled over the roar of the engine. The Augusta took off and vanished in the dark sky above.

The cruise missile's proximity fuse armed and exploded fifty yards from the fleeing boat. The boat started moving, and the few extra yards it traveled saved it from being destroyed. But the explosion was still violent and a wave so intense and powerful shook the boat so violently that the radar that picked it up went offline as well as the communication link. The wave threw the blond mercenary into the wall, knocking him out cold. The other mercenary driving the boat only suffered a broken thumb. Both of Chandra's wrists were broken and her arm was dislocated. The pain caused her to lose consciousness.

"Scorpion . . . Scorpion!" yelled the mercenary. "Come in . . . do you read me? Over. I repeat. This is Blue Rock. Come in . . . over!" Tossing the CB to the floor, he did the only thing he could do head to shore. He knew the missile came from the Navy ship, and he was certain he'd be safe in a populated area. Without any lighting, he looked out the window to see if there was any more danger. He was so keyed up when his cell phone rang that he forgot all about Scorpion passing the phone to Felix so he could talk to the girl. He quickly picked up the cell phone, fumbling with it as he kept his hand down on the throttle. "Scorpion!" he shrieked into the phone once he got it to his ear. "We were just attacked by that ship. We picked it up on the radar, but we have a little damage. I'm heading to dock at Bayside. The girl is still with us, but as soon as I get the call from Felix, I'll take care of her. Will we be meeting at the same spot? Scorpion, are you there?" He cursed when he heard static and he quickly placed the phone in his pocket. He then yelled out for his partner while scanning the sky as the boat strained to keep moving.

"What?" yelled Walters aboard the helicopter as he headed toward the site where the cruise missile had exploded.

"I said we missed! As soon as the missile blew, our radar picked up the boat fleeing the area a second before impact, but it still set off the proximity fuse. Right now we're tracking it . . . wait, hold on," said Lieutenant Atkins.

Walters stuck his head into the cockpit between the pilot and copilot. *How in the hell did they miss? This is the U.S. Navy,* he thought. Everything was pitch black and he knew the pilot

was flying with night vision. He was about to
ask the pilot a question, but Atkins' voice came
through the mic that was built into the helmet
he was wearing.

"Agent Walters, I'm about to switch you to
your boss, and yes, it's a secure line." That was
all he said before the line went dead, then a few
tones and beeps. Walters had a bad feeling that
something was wrong. The helicopter was flying
only two hundred feet above the water. As he
looked to his left, the door gunner strapped on
an M-60 machine gun and smiled back at him.
*What did they pay these guys to stand in the
doorway of a speeding helicopter as it banked
and turned heading God knows where?* Walters
thought. He hated every second on the helicopter and he prayed that it would soon be all over.
Finally the call came through.

"Stanley, you there?" yelled Troublefield.

"Yeah, it's me," Walters yelled, hating the
fact that Troublefield was somewhere in
Washington . . . nice, warm, and relaxed while
he was playing Double-07.

"We just picked up a call from the boat."

"We missed!"

"Yes, I know, but let me finish. Scorpion is
not on the boat. He's moved up his time to hit
the island. Just a few seconds ago we picked
up a call about a chopper nearly hitting a Coast

Guard cutter that was running with its lights out. When they tried to contact the chopper, it didn't answer and it was heading straight for the island."

"Do we know if he's on the helicopter or not? And what about the boat?"

"I got the Coast Guard going to Bayside. If possible, they'll take them alive. But the Navy tells me that they can track the chopper, and they're doing that as we speak. The one you're on has some kind of air-to-air missiles to handle the job."

"Joe, I didn't sign up for this shit!" Walters yelled and fell to his knees as the SH-60F banked to the right nearly rolling on it's side. Walters struggled to his feet and noticed the door gunner taking the safety off his M-60.

"You might wanna strap in, sir. We're going into combat mode!" yelled the door gunner. Walters quickly took his advice.

"Are you sure this is a good idea, Joe? Hell, we almost . . ." He then lowered his voice. "We could've gotten that hostage killed. I'm damn glad it missed."

Troublefield grunted. "Listen, Stanley, I can't tie up this line. Call me when Scorpion is dead."

"Joe . . . wait . . . " Static came over the line before he got the chance to ask Troublefield how they were going to explain to the hostage that they'd never tried to free her. But as he sat in the back of the H-60F, he knew something was fishy about how they spotted Scorpion's helicopter. For one, it was unusual for the Coast Guard to be out with no lights, so that meant Troublefield knew much more than he was willing to share. Well, at least he now knew that Scorpion was out there flying, doing who knows what. He keyed his voice mic and asked the copilot if the heli- copter had been spotted. The copilot replied no, but said they had it on the radar. The plan was to stay low and catch them heading back to Miami. This time, even with a warning, the helicopter would not escape that Mach 3 speeding missile. Walters looked at his watch. It was six forty-two.

As soon as Felix got off the phone with the hysterical mercenary, he quickly called Menage and told him that Chandra was still alive and heading to Bayside. He left out the part about the missile. Felix stood up and looked at the helicopter slowly land on his pad as some of his men drove up with the coke to be loaded. His cell phone chimed.

"Yes," he said calmly.

It was Scorpion. Since he thought Felix was still in Miami, he told him that he could pick up his girl at the airport in Homestead. Felix could have had his bodyguards take him out now since he had them hidden in the bushes next to the helipad, but Chandra wasn't safe yet and Scorpion still had the upper hand. He balled up his fists as the last crate of coke was loaded onto the helicopter. The helicopter then quickly lifted into the air, turned its nose down and headed back toward Miami with all its lights out. Felix watched it as it faded from view. He lit a cigar and sat down. It was useless to call Menage now because he knew that no matter what, he'd want to do it his way. Felix made a promise to find out Scorpion's identity, but until then, he could only wait.

The 110-foot Coast Guard cutter was at wide-open throttle as it crashed through the waves, pursuing the mercenaries. Water washed over the sailor at the bow as he sat behind a fifty-caliber machine gun with a box full of ammo.

The mercenary pulled the boat up to the dock miles away. He cut off the engine as it floated into its private slot at the pier. Seeing the deckhand standing nearby, ready to secure the boat, he then grabbed his Glock G30 and went below deck. His partner was sitting on the floor dazed, holding a towel to the gash above his eye. Placing the pistol in his waist holster he quickly found something to put on the naked girl.

"Get up, man," he said. The blond mercenary slowly got to his feet. "We have to move fast. Go up and help the deckhand tie us up. I'll be up in a second with the girl."

The blond mercenary pulled out an H&K Mark 23 pistol fitted with a silencer and a laser sight. He slowly made his way to the upper deck. He was glad it was dark and that the spot they had at the pier wasn't that well lit. Next to their boat was a huge sport cruiser. He checked quickly to see if there was anyone aboard.

"Where is the regular deckhand?" said the blond mercenary, gripping the deadly H&K Mark 23 behind his back as the huge baldheaded deckhand tied up the boat.

"Called in sick about an hour ago".

The blond mercenary looked him over quickly, dirty pants, a pair of old deck shoes and he wore the regular Bayside dock shirt. He then relaxed the grip on his pistol and bent over to toss the man the stern line. He again turned to look at the sport cruiser to make sure no one was aboard. He would enjoy placing a round right between the black man's eyes once his job was done. He heard a bump, and then saw his partner emerge from below with the woman over his shoulder. He still hoped he could get a good piece of her before they killed her.

"Hey, should I call a doctor or something?" asked the deck hand holding the stern line with one hand.

The blond mercenary, with his H&K Mark 23, quickly spun around and pointed the pistol at the deckhand. "Just mind your fucking own, man! She's just had too much to drink, that's all!"

The deckhand dropped the line and threw up his hands, taking a step back. "Hey, I . . . I don't want no trouble."

The mercenary laid Chandra down on the deck. She was still unconscious. He grabbed his partner. "Relax, will you!" He then looked at the deckhand. "Go ahead and tie us up. We're all just a little jumpy tonight, that's all," he said and flashed a fake smile.

The blond mercenary started to pull in the stern line that had fallen into the water. Suddenly, his partner gasped as he stumbled backward into him, nearly knocking him overboard. "Hey, man, what the fuck . . . " he said fighting to keep from falling over. At first he thought his partner had simply slipped, but he looked down and saw blood. "Fuck!" he said looking at his partner crumpled at his feet with blood oozing out the back of his head. His H&K Mark 23 was nearly a foot away. Before he could even blink, his eyes focused on the red laser coming from the stern of the sport cruiser. His mind went into overdrive. It had to be the FBI Hostage Rescue Team. Well, at least he would live. He slowly raised his hands as what looked to be the deckhand jumped on board. Pain and shock ran though his already throbbing head as the deckhand smacked him across the face with his own pistol. He fell to his knees in his partner's blood. Someone else jumped on board and rushed to the girl. He shook his head and saw stars.

"Listen, fool, ain't talkin' white no mo'. Where ya boss man at?" Dough-Low said towering over the blond mercenary. Menage knelt next to Chandra's limp body with tears in his eyes. He examined her busted lip, closed eye, and dried blood around her nose and mouth.

"Come on, baby girl," he whispered as he carefully gathered her up in his arms. When he stood up, her head fell back and her arm hung lifelessly out of its socket. His sweetheart was broken. It took everything he had within him not to cry out and curse God.

"Get her out of here, 'Nage. I think somebody comin'," Dough-Low said looking out to sea at the speeding Coast Guard cutter with its lights flashing. He didn't know if it was after the boat or if someone had called them. Either way he wasn't about to find out. Menage hurried off the boat as fast as he could.

"Hey, sucka, you gonna talk or what?" Dough-Low asked as he kicked the blond mercenary in his stomach. The mercenary fell on his side. Before he could reply, Dough-Low shot him four times, in both elbows and knees. The mercenary yelled out in pain and Dough-Low kicked him in his mouth, knocking out his front top and bottom teeth and busting his lip. "Scuffed up my shoes, muthafucka. Now die slowly. Yeah, it's true! Don't ever fuck wit' a black man and somethin' he loves." Dough-Low reached into his pocket and pulled out a small object as he jumped off the boat. Tossing it over the rail, he turned and hauled ass down the pier, licking off shots from his .380 in case anyone was being nosy. As he made it to the gate, the boat erupted into a ball of flame, lifting it twenty feet out of the water. By the time it came back down onto the water, it had split in half. The Coast Guard cutter slowly pulled into the area at a safe distance with its spotlight focused on the smoking boat. Dough-Low calmly pulled off in his SUV as Menage sat in the back holding his girl in his arms, tears running down his face.

Dough-Low didn't speak. Instead he cracked the sunroof and lit up an L as they made their getaway.

Scorpion flew the speeding helicopter at two hundred feet as it crossed the still black water. In the distance, he could see the coastline of Miami. Everything was going as planned; he had the drugs and Felix was on his way to meet his maker. Once that was done, he would collect the four million dollars. As for the two mercenaries with him, they would be easily disposed of. And the two fools with the girl would be waiting for a ride that would never show up. The only loose end would be Myrmidon. It was something about Myrmidon that Scorpion didn't like, or maybe it was that he feared him. He slowly banked the heavy loaded helicopter to the left and dropped down to a hundred feet. He then saw a glare out of the corner of his eye. He cursed himself for leaving on the collision lights and he hit the switch. Miami was now only four miles away.

***

Walters watched through his tinted visor as the air-to-air, state of the art heat-seeking missile headed toward the slow moving helicopter. Even when it veered left, the missile followed. Moments before, Walters had held his breath as the helicopter flew over the aircraft that carried him. It all seemed like a game as the pilot lined up the fleeing helicopter and fired the deadly missile. When the helicopter again made a feeble attempt to dodge the missile, Walters again held his breath, but this time he would not be let down. The missile hit the helicopter dead center, causing its fuel to catch fire. The helicopter exploded in midair and burst into a huge flame, causing Walters to cringe even behind his visor. The dismantled helicopter, still on fire, fell to the sea. When Walters and the two pilots reached the area where the aircraft went down, they looked at each other in wonderment as a white powdery mist floated through the atmosphere. Walters immediately knew that it was cocaine. There was no sign of life down below. "Clear," he said to himself. He then asked the pilot to put him through to the Coast Guard and hoped the hostage could be rescued without any bloodshed.

Myrmidon looked at his watch. It was dark, and he wasn't willing to take a risk and turn on the small light. Scorpion called no more than twenty minutes earlier, telling him that Felix was on his way to the airport. He was on the second floor overlooking the abandoned airfield. To his left, about three hundred yards away, was the front gate. The plan was for Felix to drive up and drop off a million dollars at the gate, tossing it out the window. "It's just you and me," he whispered and kissed the stock of his R-25 Stoner Sniper rifle. He then closed his eyes as the guilt hit him about the girl. He knew she was as good as dead when she was left on the boat with the other two mercenaries. A limo drove up to the gate, locking its back wheels and breaking his train of thought. The back window slowly slid down. Myrmidon quickly placed his greased up eye to the scope of his rifle and lined up his target.

As the black non-reflective barrel stuck out of the broken window, he centered the crosshairs on the temple of his target. He placed his finger on the trigger and exhaled. The crosshairs dropped but were still on target. Close to five hundred yards away, at the other end of the airfield, lying in the high uncut grass was a former U.S. Marine sniper, now working for the CIA. He was armed with a deadly hi-tech M82A1.50 caliber Berretta rifle fitted with a special thermal image scope. He exhaled and pulled the trigger, sending a laser beam of light toward his target. Something flashed in Myrmidon's scope, breaking his focus. He quickly looked up to find the source. A subsonic round was three seconds behind the light. Myrmidon never had the chance to finish his thoughts, as the round tore through the top of his cheek, destroying his cornea and sclera. Then within a fraction of a second, his parietal skull plate exploded out the back of his head, vaporizing his cerebral cortex. The round was later found by CIA agents, embedded thirty feet away and five inches deep in solid steel. Myrmidon now lay headless with his finger on the trigger of his rifle. The limo was CIA, and if Myrmidon did get a shot off, it would have hit a dummy. The former Marine stood up in full body camo and said, "One shot, one kill."

Later That Night
USS Reuben James

"Some night, huh, Lieutenant?" asked Walters to Atkins as his ship headed back to Norfolk with new orders.

"Yeah, you can say that. It seems that the powers that be have given my men a little Rand

R, but you and I both know it'll be hear no evil, speak no evil, see no evil." They both laughed, and Walters' mind went back to the crash site of the helicopter. There were a few floating body parts, but as soon as the flare went out, the sharks came. It was amazing how they could smell a drop of blood miles away. It was a waste of time and fuel to stay at the site, and the pilot headed back to the ship.

Since the CIA wanted Scorpion and his team at all costs, they didn't tell the local police that nine times out of ten, it was Menage who caused the ruckus at Bayside. As far as Walters was concerned, he wished he could give the guy a medal or some thing, but for now it was back to D.C. He gazed at the coastline of Miami as the ship moved at a slow but steady speed. He might as well enjoy the ride; his seasickness had passed, and he now had time to be away from Troublefield. He ran his hand over his thin brown hair, zipped up his life vest, and looked up at the countless stars above.

Chapter 2

Passion in my life

A Month Later,
May Thursday-8:29 p.m.
Coral Gables
University of Miami

"I can't believe this," Dwight said sitting on the hood of his BMW 7 series facing Menage, who was sitting on his S600.

Dwight waited for two college girls to walk to their dorm before continuing. "You mean to tell me that the entire time I thought your narrow ass was in a coma, that you were on the island with Felix? And why didn't you come to me about Chandra, man?"

Dwight crossed his arms as the ticking of the BMW engine eased the silence between them in the parking lot.

"Yo, man, shit was fucked up. I didn't know who to trust. Hell, I still don't know who tried to set me up," Menage said pulling up the collar on his sky blue Versace flight suit. "My word, yo, I was gonna say fuck the fame and just be wit' Chandra, but she ain't the same—won't even talk to me no more." He let out a deep breath while fumbling with the Mercedes emblem on the hood. He tried to avoid Dwight's gaze because he didn't want him to see the pain that was still burning inside him inside. "How Tina doin'?"

"Fine. She nearly fell out when I told her I was coming to meet you. She'll have a fit later when I tell her what Chandra went through. Hey, man, you know how to reach me if you need anything."

Menage rubbed his face and spoke through his jeweled hands. "I'ma be okay," he said and dropped his hand lightly on the hood of his car. "Yo, we still got a goal to reach, right?" He forced a platinum smile.

"So you really getting back in the mix to reach that mill?" Dwight asked.

Menage looked around the parking lot. Money would never fill the void that Chandra had left. "Yeah. I'ma go to the shop in the morning. Ain't called DJ yet, but I'll talk to him when I see him."

"He's kind of taken root in your spot."

"Well, he can just unroot his ass, 'cause I'm back! And I ain't up for no bullshit. I respect the nigga for holdin' it down and all that, but this is business!" Menage said trying to keep his cool.

Dwight waited for a second before he spoke. "Well, just call me when you get to the shop and I'll swing by with your cut on what was made while you were gone."

"What's the deal wit' the DB-7?"

"I had DJ get rid of it."

Menage glanced at his Bulova. It was a little after eight thirty. "Look, I have to go by the salon and catch up on some paper work," said Dwight pulling out his keys. "But like I said, we still a team, man." Dwight gave Menage a pound then bumped shoulders with him.

"You still my nigga," Menage said. "Let's do what we started out to do." Menage watched Dwight pull off with his system knocking. And just as he got into his S600, Tony called from the shop. "Holla," Menage said as the seat of his Benz slid into a programmed position.

"A plan B just came in wit' a Q45." Plan B was a code Menage had his men use while stealing cars. They would go to a dealership with fake ID. Since the salesperson would be riding along for the test drive, the greed for a

sale would never cause him or her to ask for
ID. The salesperson would drive off the lot
with one of the workers who played the game
as if they were really trying to buy the car. The
salesperson would be taken to a setup house
or any place where he or she could be fooled.
Once they pulled up to the house or switching
spot, the salesperson would get out to let the
worker drive. It would only take two seconds
for the worker to jump over into the driver's
seat and pull off, and since no weapon was
ever used nor the salesperson forced out of the
car, the perpetrator would only face an auto
theft charge if caught.

"Who did it?"

"Wally. He did it in the parking lot at Burger
King."

"Okay. You know what to do. I'll see you in
the morning." Menage started up his S600
and the rims started to spin. "CD four, song
two, volume mid, bass max." Tupac's "Against
All Odds" shook the Benz as it slowly pulled out
of the parking lot. Clutching the oak steering
wheel with one hand, he reflected on his life
as he pushed his ride up to cruising speed. He
knew how hard life could be. He remembered
the roach-infested projects and having to heat
up the bath water on the stove to take a bath and
then rushing to get in the tub before the water

got cold. He remembered the welfare stamps, the hot nights with nothing but a fan to blow more heat around. He remembered nights of rubbing alcohol on his chest just to feel that cool breeze for a few seconds. Before he even bought his first pair of Air Ones with his dirty money, he took care of Mom Dukes first. She now laid her head on silk pillows and walked around on plush carpet.

More than half of the girls who fucked him were caught up by the sight of his caddy truck with the gulwing doors, the roofless Legend or his iced-out wrist and neck. It all seemed senseless to Menage now, but what else was there? Chandra did a good job of making him realize that love was a waste of time. Yeah, she did a good job of that.

By the time he made it back to the hood in Northwest Miami, it had started to rain. At the corner of Sixty-second, he ran into a store to buy a six-pack of Heineken. Sipping from the bottle with a Glock-19 in his lap, he cruised around the hood trying to force Chandra from his mind. From pain to joy and joy to pain, his life resembled the single windshield wiper moving back and forth across the front window. Menage thought about swinging by Club Bounce Back, but the thought of being around a lot of folks didn't sit well with him.

Turning down the system as he cruised down 103rd, he made a call on the car phone by voice command.

"Hello?"

"Yeah, is Irish in?"

"Hold on a sec. May I ask who's calling?"

"Menage."

Seconds later, Irish's sexy voice came on the line.

"Hey, Boo, what's up? Ain't seen you in a while."

"You know how it rolls. I'm tryin' to see you tonight. What's up?"

"Man, hey, I got company right now, but he ain't staying all night. Come on over and play like you my cousin and just chill with my girl Passion until he leave, all right?"

Menage knew the game and he'd rather play the side he was on than be a nigga blinded by pussy. "Yeah, I'm on my way. Tell your man to make it wet for me and I'll take care of your needs."

"Bye, fool." Irish giggled before she hung up. The rain finally stopped as Menage headed for I-95 to Hollywood in Broward County. He kept the CD on repeat as Ashanti's "Rain on Me" filled the Benz. Irish would erase Chandra from his mind and heart. Sex and money, chrome rims and . . . "My world," he said to himself, forcing his motto deeper into his mind as the big body Benz rolled onto the freeway. "I was born by myself and I'll die by myself!"

Menage slowly backed his S600 into a parking space in front of Irish's apartment next to a chromed out midnight black Lexus ES-300. Adjusting his holster under his arm, he got out and set the alarm. Irish answered the door on the third knock.

"What's up, boy?" she asked grinning, rocking a pair of blue, skintight terry cloth dollhouse side zip shorts with a matching tight fitting corset top. "Mmmm, I see you brought me some Heinekens. Come on in," she said. Stepping into the blue tinted living room, Menage nodded his head at Irish's friend sitting on the couch nursing a bottle of Bud Light. "Passion in the back, okay? It's the second door on the left," Irish said over her shoulder walking toward the kitchen. Making his exit, he walked down the hall playing the role of Irish's cousin. He tapped on the door. "Come in, it's open." As soon as he opened the door, scented candles filled his nostrils. Menage couldn't deny his excitement when he stepped into the bedroom and found Passion lying on the queen-sized bed on her stomach with her legs parted talking on the phone. He stood there for a few seconds, looking at her thick thunder thighs and heart-shaped ass. The short green and black teddy with a matching thong made him bite his lip. "You can close the door," she said halfway turning over, causing her reddish brown shoulder length hair to bounce about. Menage closed the door and moved to a plastic chair in the corner by the bed, his eyes traveling over her mahogany colored skin. He sat down and tried to look around the room as she talked on the phone, but his eyes kept going back to her body. Now with a side view, he swore he could sit a cup on her ass if she was standing . . . He hoped Irish's company didn't stay too long, because he couldn't wait to unzip those shorts and suck on her tasty tits . . . *Damn, Passion had a phat ass, and a smile to match!* He imagined having Irish and Passion in a three-way.

"Girl, will you stop being so damn nosy? Yes, I gots me some company," Passion said still talking on the phone, doing her best to ignore Menage. "No, I'm not telling you who it is, so don't ask. Yeah, heifer, you say that now, but your ass will be calling me to take you to Social Service next week. And I got a Lexus, 'cause I work. But look, I'll call you back. Yes, girl, yes. All right, bye." Hanging up the phone, she moved around on the bed to face Menage and rested on her elbows with her forearms crossed. He received a full view of her soft-looking cleavage as she swung her small feet back and forth in the air.

"You just getting here?" she asked causing the light to glisten off her red luscious lips.

"Yeah," he said realizing she looked nothing like the scared girl he first saw at the park.

"Man, you're brave to come while Lazy Dee still here. But I guess you just as crazy as Irish is, huh?"

"Nah, but your man . . . he's the one that's crazy!"

She stopped swinging her feet. "Oh, you remember that day, huh?" Menage could hear the nervousness in her voice.

"Yeah." Menage would never forget that day at Liberty Square Park with Dough-Low.

"Well, I don't mess with him no more. He used to . . . well, I just had to leave him alone and I'm doing much better without his ass. And I model . . . well, if you call posing for Black Tail modeling."

"Say word?" he asked wishing he could see the real deal.

"Word," she said giggling. "It was just a one time thing. This guy saw me on the beach and made me an offer. One good enough for me to get a used car and have a few dollars left over. They still callin', but I'm not really into that plus I'm supposed to start at Florida A&M next year."

"That's straight, but did you really pose?" he asked wishing he could see the pictures.

"Yes, boy, and no I don't keep the pictures around," she said blushing. "Did you ride your bike?"

"Nah, I drove," he said willing himself to gaze into her hazel eyes.

"Do you mind if I ask you how old you are?" she asked resting her chin on her folded arms.

"Twenty-four. What about you, if you don't mind?" he asked smiling, revealing his platinum fronts.

"I'm nineteen, no kids, I don't smoke, and drugs is a no-no. You don't get high, do you?" She shocked herself with her own question; he wasn't there to see her but she hoped he said no anyway.

"I smoke weed and I drink, but only when I go out. I don't get drunk like that."

"That's cool. But you don't do no powder or any of that mess, do you?"

"Hell, naw." He managed to look past her raised shoulders and check out her thighs and ass when she rubbed her eyes. "You tired?"

"No, something was just in my eye. Look, I know I'm asking a million questions, but do you have a permit for that thang?"

"Say what!"

"Boy, I'm talking about that gun, not your um . . . " She laughed shyly.

"Hey, you seem like a nice girl and all, but I take it you're single."

"Why you say that?"

"Because if I was your man, I'd sure as hell be with you now."

Passion was stunned. "Is that right? Well, yes I'm single. Too bad you're not." *Damn that slipped,* she thought to herself. She changed the subject before he could reply. "What kind of music do you listen to?" she asked squeezing her thighs together.

"Mostly reggae, dancehall, and R&B. I like rap when I'm driving."

Neither of them spoke for a few seconds. "I'll go see what's taking Irish so long. Be right back." She slid off the bed, slipping her small feet into a pair of slippers. When she stood up, Menage shook his head at the sight of her body. She was about five foot seven and thick as hell. He wondered if she was kin to Benita. He let out a low inaudible moan as she walked toward the door. Her butt cheeks jiggled and shook, and the short teddy stopped at the curve of her ass. Menage wondered why she tossed a towel over her back. He wished he could be waiting for her in that bed buck naked. But or tonight, it was Irish and her deep throating skills and glove tight pussy.

"Bad news, Menage," Passion said coming back into the room. She tossed him a small piece of paper before he could ask her what was up. She sat on the edge of the bed with her chin resting in the palms of her hands as he read the note that was written on the paper.

> *Passion,*
> *Girl, Lazy come up with some bullshit about getting a room and I couldn't come back to tell ya'll Tell 'Nage I'm sorry. Ya'll have fun! See ya in the morn.*
> *Irish*

Passion looked at the time. It was just after twelve, another night alone. Menage handed her back the note. "Sorry," she said softly, balling it up and throwing it in the trash.

"Sorry about what? She told us to have fun, right?" he asked.

Passion looked at him. She was physically attracted to him, but . . . *Oh, what the hell,* she thought.

"Hey, Passion, when's the last time you had your feet massaged?"

"Never," she said with a straight face.

"No, I'm for real."

"I'm for real, too! I've never had my feet massaged." She never even had her back massaged, but she decided not to mention it.

Menage slid his chair up closer to the bed. "Well, this is what I'd like to do. I want you to get me some oil and put on some music and I'ma see if I can be the first to massage those sexy feet of yours," he said, rubbing his hands together and smiling at her.

"Boy, stop playing with me," she giggled.

"I'm serious, Passion. I really wanna do it. And I'll need a towel."

Passion got everything he had asked for. After turning on her CD player, they agreed on R. Kelly's *12 Play*. Seconds later, she gasped as his finger rubbed the heels of her feet that were now resting in his lap. She leaned halfway back, resting on her elbows as "Your Body's Callin'" filled the room. Passion breathed deeply as

Menage's hands caressed her feet, massaging warm oil into her skin. "Your feet are sexy," he said admiring them.

"Th-thank you . . . ooooh." *Dang, that slipped,* she thought to herself.

"Something wrong?" he asked looking up to see her bottom lip tucked in tightly.

"Uh, no. It just . . . it just feels so nice. I never had anyone do me like this before." She was amazed at the time he spent on making her feel good and the time he took to learn more about her. As the moments passed, she started to open up more to him.

"Menage, I need to tell you something," she said unable to look into his eyes.

"What is it?" he whispered as his working fingers sent chills all over her body.

"My ex. He used to beat me real bad and—"

"His way of showing his so-called love was to beat you and cause that mark on your back?"

"Yes. How did you see it?" She pulled her feet away, surprised he didn't try to hold onto them.

"I've been studying your body since I first walked through that door, Passion. And I hope you're not comparing me to your ex. I'd never put my hands on you in anger," he said looking into her eyes.

"What's going to happen between us, Menage? I don't wanna do anything to make you not respect me in the morning, so I need to—"

"Give me your feet, Passion, and close your eyes," he said cutting her off again.

"Huh?"

"Give me your feet and close your eyes. I'll make it right for you."

She slowly slid her feet back into his lap. Her eyes closed as soon as he touched them again. "Keep your eyes closed and enjoy," he said before leaning forward and flicking his tongue back and forth between her toes.

"Menage, please," she moaned as she opened her eyes and watched the toes of her left foot vanish into his mouth. "Oh, baby," she said falling on her back, squeezing her thighs together. "Oh, Menage, it feels so good." Passion ran her fingers through her hair. The lights remained on and neither of them seemed to mind.

"Tell me when to stop. Okay, Passion?" Menage said licking her ankles. Passion could only nod her head as she felt him placing wet kisses on her legs. He gently bit her inner thigh down by her knee, causing her to cry out his name. Crouching down, he parted her legs and lifted them. He sucked on the back of her thighs as his hands slowly slid up to her hips. He could see the damp spot on her thong and saw that she kept the area well trimmed. He slowly began twirling his tongue in circles near her inner thigh.

"Stop, please stop," she said pushing his head away. She sat up on the bed and feared that he'd be angry, but she was surprised to see him moving back to the chair.

"I'm sorry. Do you want me to leave? If you do I'll under stand," he said softly.

She quickly shook her head no. "Can you t-take that g-gun off and your shirt? I want to see more of you, please," she said fumbling with her fingers.

He stood up, took off his holster and then the top half of the flight suit. "Tell me when to stop," he said looking into her eyes as he took off his medallion. He kicked off his Air Ones then slowly started to unzip the lower half of his flight suit. Passion's eyes traveled over his scarred chest, chiseled arms, and well toned legs. She marveled at his smooth looking body. Her heart raced and her sex began to throb as he stood at the edge of her bed in a pair of silk boxers that did nothing to hide his erection. "Wait. Stop," she said when his fingers slid under the waistband. There was no doubt in her mind that she wanted him. J-Money had never made her feel this way. He only filled her with fear. She thought it would be special when he took her virginity, but instead he had beaten her with his fists for getting blood on his new bed. He would call her a bitch as he grunted over her and beat her if she didn't cum when he did. He told her his dick was too good to be inside her sorry ass raw. Thank God for that; she'd have nightmares had she ever given birth to his child. He even made her have sex with him in front of his friends and busted her lip when she claimed she had cramps after he tried to force her to fuck one of them. He pulled his gun on her on another occasion, sending her fleeing down the street naked back to their apartment because she had forgotten to bring along his dog on a short trip to the corner store. Irish finally made her realize that love didn't equal a busted lip. Passion was scared of J-Money, and the only way she got away from him was by telling him she had AIDS. It was a sick lie, but she was dying a slow death by staying with him. He nearly broke her shoulder when he hit her with a bat, kicking her out of the apartment. Now she sat alone in a bedroom with a man she'd just met. In a few hours he had her feeling things she'd never thought were possible. She slowly sat up on her knees, looking into his soft brown eyes as the CD player changed to a slow relaxing tune. She reached down and touched the hem of her green teddy.

"Tell me when to stop," she said with a sly grin as she pulled the teddy up over her head. She enjoyed his eyes roaming over her body. She reached behind her back to unsnap her bra and removed it. She began sliding her thong down when Menage whispered for her to stop.

"Can I touch you, Passion?"

She nodded her head yes and backed away from him until she fell onto her back. Her hands crossed over her breasts.

"Please tell me when to stop," he said lying next to her as his tongue darted out to lick her right breast underneath her left arm. She instantly lifted her arms and placed her hands on the back of his head, pressing his face to her breasts.

"Mmmm," she moaned as his tongue circled her nipple. His right hand squeezed her left nipple now, while the other hand moved in a slow circle around her belly button. J-Money was far from her mind now, as she no longer compared him to Menage. Menage's hand moved to the top of her thong and slowly slid under it. His touch caused her hips to jerk forward. She reached for his wrist and slid his hand further down toward her sex. She cried out his name when his fingers moved over her outer lips. Menage eased two fingers inside of her wet opening and slowly started to please her.

"Menage, you make it feel so nice." Passion couldn't stay still. Grabbing his face and bringing it to hers as his fingers slid in and out of her, she looked into his eyes. "Don't stop," she whispered.

"Can I kiss you, Passion?"

She closed her eyes, wishing she had told him her other secrets. J-Money had never brought her to orgasm. Sure, she did it herself when he was out on the block and also by . . . well, she knew she couldn't share that info with Menage. Her arms locked around his neck when his tongue slid into her mouth, and she let out a soft moan each time his fingers entered her.

"Do you want me, Passion?" he managed to ask as they deeply kissed.

"Mmm, aah," she moaned as her smooth hands traveled down his back and tugged at his boxers. She began chanting and muttering something over and over, but he couldn't make it out until they stopped kissing. He pulled down his boxers and pressed his penis into her body. Passion's hot breath warmed his neck as she spoke.

"Make me cum. I want . . . I need you to be in me, Menage," she said quickly. She raised her hips and he slid her thong down her legs, removing it. Menage looked at her V-shaped pubic hairs, the shape of her stomach, the curve of her hips, the tiny bumps around her nipples, her sexy lips, her eyes, her collar bone, and he promised himself that he would be familiar with every inch of her body. But why? Surely this was a one-night stand. Fuck her and leave. No, that wasn't what he wanted.

"J-Money used to force me to have oral sex, but I'll do it for you if—"

"Shhh, don't ever speak his name again, Passion," he said before moving between her thick thighs. "I just wanna touch you all over." He began to rub her breasts. Moments later, her entire body was on fire as he was on top of her, kissing the side of her neck while her hands slid over his bare penis. Menage felt her fingers squeezing him as she rubbed the head of his penis up and down between her wet lips. "Passion, that feels so damn good," he said knowing that all he simply had to do was thrust forward to be inside her. Passion placed her legs up on his hips.

"Baby, the condoms are on the table, but I wanna . . . " She paused, feeling her own secretions trickle down between her ass cheeks.

"Wanna what?" Menage asked sliding his hand between her ass cheeks and feeling her wetness. She was hot.

"Mmmm, I just wanna feel you inside me with nothing between us. I just want to feel what it's . . . oh, my! Yesss!" she cried out as he slowly started penetrating her. When he was deep inside her he lost his composure, calling out her name.

"Passion!" he yelled pressing down harder. She ran her fingers over his sweating ass as their lips locked again. He clenched her hair, kissing her deeply, and her sex gripped tightly around his penis. Without pulling out, he started to grind and rotate his hips, causing his penis to twirl deeply within her. She broke away from his kiss and called out his name. Locking her legs around his waist now, she dug her nails into his ass, causing him to go deeper. He continued to marinate inside her as her hand eased down to where they were joined. Menage began to moan when she touched his sac. Slowly he withdrew from her. Her body moved forward toward his and then she relaxed. Neither knew nor cared how it started, and he slid back in and out of her wetness with long, steady strokes.

"Aw, baby, yes, yes, yes," she panted as she felt his strokes start to quicken.

"Stop me, Passion," he said getting up on his elbows.

"Make me cum," she said gripping his shoulders. "Do it! Please!"

Menage closed his eyes. Ever since he'd lost Chandra, nothing mattered. He put Passion's left leg over his arm as he picked up the pace. She met every stroke with a soft whimper as her breasts bounced with each smack of his hips slamming into her body. Passion closed her eyes as he pumped steadily, causing the bed to start squeaking. It was feeling so good that he didn't realize she was biting his arm until he moved it away from her mouth. He positioned her right leg and she placed her hands around his waist and looked down at what he was doing to her. She moaned each time he slammed his penis into her, stretching her sex. Her inner walls clung to him as he pumped her. She watched the flexing of his stomach, the sweat trickling down his body onto hers. Passion wanted him to make her cum. She needed it. She soon found herself lying on her side as Menage slid into her from behind.

"Is this what you want, baby?" he panted.

"Yes, Menage, yes," she replied as their bodies thrashed together. "*Asi bueno*, baby!"

They somehow ended up on the floor, her riding him wildly, as if she hadn't a care in the world. She started to feel the way she always felt whenever she pleased herself or . . . anyway, she was feeling it now. Her breasts started to hurt from the constant flopping up and down, but there was no way that she was going to stop.

"Menage, I'm getting ready to do it, gonna do it, gonna do it. Ooooh!" She bounced on him as she started to nut and then leaned forward and lay her hands flat on the floor as she began to grind her body into his. Without a thought, she slid off of his still erect penis and began running her tongue over it.

"Passion, wait!" he said reaching for her.

"No!" I want to do it," she said putting it in her mouth and looking dead into his eyes. She began to blow him and each time she raised her head, his hips moved forward, seeking her mouth. "Mmmm, mmmm, mmmm," she purred, and licked and slurped his dick like candy.

"How do you want me to please you?" she asked as she flicked her tongue around the head of his penis.

"G-get on your hands and knees," he said wiping the sweat from his face.

Passion crawled toward the middle of the room. "Like this?" she asked looking over her shoulder as he came up behind her.

"Spread your legs farther apart."

She moved her legs farther apart and reached for a pillow to rest her head upon. "Watch," she said as she reached between her thighs and started masturbating. Her fingers became moist, and she reached for his penis and coated it with her wetness. "Take it, please, Menage. I want you to cum." She balanced herself on her elbows, arching her ass up higher. Five minutes later, he had her cumming for the second time as he drilled her from behind. She yelled out his name, urging him to cum with her, telling him how good it felt. Menage threw his head back and continued to fuck Passion. His thrust became so strong that she slowly fell to her stomach. Her body quivered and she started pounding her fist on the floor. Pulling out, he pressed his penis down between her ass cheeks and onto her back as she rotated her hips and cried out. Ignoring her cum-coated back, she rolled over and pulled him down onto her. They kissed for what seemed like eternity, their hands roaming each other's bodies.

"Mmm, thank you, baby, thank you," she cried kissing his face. Passion never wanted to let him go, but she had to face reality. *It's just sex and nothing more,* she thought as she wiped him down with a warm rag.

"You okay?" he asked later as he finished putting on his clothes.

"Yeah," she lied. *You got what you wanted, so leave.*

He put on his medallion and watched her put new sheets on the bed. She couldn't even look his way. "Do you want me to call you? Can I call you? I'd like to see you again."

Her heart stopped and she told another lie to protect her heart. "Boy, we both know this is a one-time affair."

Menage's mouth dropped in shock. He was being turned down. He wanted to tell her how he really wanted to get to know her better, regardless of the fact that they had sex so soon. He felt stupid as he headed for the door. Passion didn't escort him out because she didn't want to see him leave. She allowed the sex they had to cloud her judgment and block her emotions. As soon as she heard the door close, she sat on the bed and started to cry. She couldn't be with Menage just for sex. She knew it would be nothing more than that, even though he did make her feel wanted. She also knew he'd never share his life with a woman who fucked and sucked his dick on the first night.

Passion stepped out of the shower minutes later and heard a knock at the door. She was certain it was Menage returning. Holding a towel to her wet body, she walked quickly to the door, planning to drop the towel once she saw him. Her beaming smile was quickly erased, and terror soon appeared on her face as she opened the door and saw J-Money standing in the door way. She covered her face with her hands, dropping the towel. "You lying bitch!" he hissed, mashing her in the face as he stepped into the apartment.

Menage couldn't believe Passion had put him off, not him, the one and only Menage Unique Legend. He felt like a sucker as he headed back to his mansion. Maybe he was feeling this way because of the pain he experienced with Chandra. Sure, Passion was fine-banging body, good sex. But that was nothing to Menage. He just didn't understand the rejection. He even made her bust a nut twice and he was gentle with her because of her past.

He reached for the cell phone on his hip, but it wasn't there. He slowed down his S600 as he hit the interior light . . . still no phone. "Damn," he said, realizing that it was still in Passion's bedroom. Making a quick U-turn, he headed back to the apartment. He started to blow the horn and have her bring it out, but he knew that would be rude, so he turned his car off and walked up to the door for the second time. He knocked and waited. He thought that maybe she was taking a shower. He turned the knob to find that the door was unlocked. He made a mental note to tell her about that not being a safe thing to do. He noticed that the light was on under her door and music was playing loudly. He knocked and slowly opened the door, and for the second time tonight he was not ready for what he saw.

Menage cringed at the sight before him. J-Money held Passion down by her neck, choking her as he raped her. The music was so loud that they didn't hear him enter the room. The bed was torn up and the night table was broken. Menage saw the blood on Passion's hands as she clawed at J-Money's face. He no longer saw Passion, but Chandra. He didn't even remember pulling out his Glock-19. J-Money didn't feel the first crack against his skull, but the second one drew blood. He rolled off of Passion and onto his back, holding his head. The music was no longer playing because J-Money had pulled the plug to the radio out of the wall when he had fallen over. He tried to pull up his pants, but Menage cocked the Glock and he froze. Passion's face was a mess, and Menage could see that she would need stitches.

"You know this bitch nigga, Passion?" he asked with the Glock-19 in a firm two-hand military grip. "Wait. I know your bitch ass." Menage realized that this man was her ex and that he was in the middle of a domestic dispute. He'd heard a lot of crazy stories about how the woman would always take up for the same sorry-ass excuse of a man who beat her. With that thought, Menage backed up a little while keeping his eye on Passion. She looked so helpless.

"Why the fuck you beatin' on the girl?"

J-Money glared at him. "Tell him, Passion, dis how we get off."

Menage looked at Passion as she lowered her head. J-Money smiled. "See, nigga, you—"

"Shut the fuck up!" Menage yelled, cutting him off. He knew that what he was about to ask was stupid, but he was in the mix. "Do you want me to leave, Passion?" She began sobbing and shook her head no.

"Bitch, what?" asked J-Money.

"Nigga, didn't I tell you to shut the fuck up? Huh?" Menage asked. He looked at Passion and told her to get dressed. She got up holding her side and got dressed as fast as she could.

"Shoot him," she said calmly.

"Passion, just get dressed. You talkin' crazy."

"No, he was going to kill me," she said standing behind him now.

"Do he have a gun?" She threw back the sheets and grabbed a chrome .357 and pointed it at J-Money.

"Passion, put the gun down now, girl!" said J-Money.

Tears ran down her bruised face as the heavy gun shook in her small hands.

Menage eyed her finger on the trigger. "Passion, you don't wanna do this. Listen to me!"

"He said it's my fault and that no man will ever respect me and I'm worthless. I don't wanna be like this no more. I'm nothing," she sobbed. Menage tightened his grip on his glock. Passion continued. "Don't nobody respect me. All I ever wanted was love." She looked at Menage. "Why did you come back?"

He looked at the cell phone on the floor and then at the .357. "I . . . I came back for you, Passion." She let his words sink in and as they did, the .357 dropped to her side. But she knew J-Money would stalk her till she died, and the thought of him touching her again made her shiver. Menage reached into his pocket and pulled out a knot of cash. He gave Passion $750.00 and told her to get in her car and leave. She picked up his cell phone and took the money. She was in such a daze that she didn't even realize Menage had taken the gun from her.

"Pull your pants up, you bitch-ass coward!" Menage said as Passion left the room. He could smoke him right now, dead in the forehead. "Nah, strip, nigga, get buck naked!"

J-Money sucked his teeth, but he did as he was told. Snatching up J-Money's clothes, Menage slowly backed up, still pointing the gun at him. "Roll over, muthafucka. You wanna take the chance to see if I'm gone, look up, but if I see your ass move, I'ma burn ya. Now plug the radio back up." The loud music filled the room, and J-Money couldn't tell if he was gone or not. Running outside, Menage found Passion sitting on the ground, crying next to her ES-300 with its busted windows and four flat tires. He scooped her up in his arms and walked quickly to his Benz. After placing her in the passenger's seat, he ran and got in on the other side. Backing out, he noticed a blue Chevy. It was J-Money's whip. Menage stopped and lowered his window. He fired three rounds from the .357 at the Chevy. Then he pulled out his Glock-19 and emptied the clip. Before burning rubber, he reached over to rub Passion's neck. She jumped at first, ducking her head as if he was going to hit her.

"It's okay, Passion. You wit' me, now. C' mere." She slowly moved toward him and rested her head on his shoulder. "I . . . I got your phone," she said. He smiled as he rubbed her back. She was now certain why he had really come back. Passion didn't know what to expect when they passed a hotel. Surely he wasn't going to take her home. That's why she held onto the money he'd given her. But when they crossed into Dade County, she remained silent. She admitted to herself that she didn't really know him that well. All she knew was that he had a nice car, money, platinum . . . and he was probably another drug dealer like J-Money. No, she couldn't compare the two; J-Money wasn't even human in her book. Passion was shocked when they pulled up to the hospital in Miami. *So this is where he'll drop me off,* she thought. When the doctor cleaned her up, she asked him if he could call her a cab. She still had the money Menage had given her, and she would get a room and make her way back home to New York.

"Why do you need a cab? My ride ain't good enough?" Menage asked walking into the room where Passion still sat up on the examining table. She couldn't believe that he had waited for her. But she was even more surprised when they later pulled up to his mansion.

"Passion, you can chill with me. It's safe here and you'll also have your own room. Okay?"

"Is this your house?"

"House no, mansion yes." He told her to sit still until he came around to open the door for her.

"Thank you so much, Menage," she whispered as he supported her on their way to the front door.

Later on in the wee hours of the morning, Menage lay on his bed looking up at the ceiling. Passion was downstairs asleep. He knew she had been through a lot so he didn't add any pressure to the situation by approaching her for sex. And more than anything, he wondered what the days ahead would bring. He still hadn't told Passion how he felt about her.

He was about to doze off when Vapor got up and went to the bedroom door growling. "Easy, boy," Menage said sitting up now. Seconds later Passion lightly knocked on the door. "Come in, its open . . . front door, boy." Vapor knew he had to leave, but he would be right back at the bedroom door when ordered. Passion came in and closed the door behind Vapor. No words were spoken as she crawled into Menage's bed. All she wore was a XXL NBA Jersey.

"I don't wanna sleep by myself. Can you please hold me?" she whispered. As she rested her body against his chest, she told him she had turned to another woman after all the abuse J-Money had put her through. Menage said he understood. She told him she needed to go back home and that she had hidden her true feelings from him because she didn't want to make a fool of herself. He shocked her when he told her he had done the same thing. She said she still needed some time to think. Menage was impressed. She was unmoved by his material items, and that drew him to her even more.

"So what do we do now?" she asked rubbing his face.

"Take it day by day. You go home and get yourself together, okay?" he replied holding her close in the dimly lit room.

"I really do like you a lot, Menage."

"I like you too, Passion, more than you may realize."

"Do you have a condom?" she asked pressing her breasts into his chest.

"Passion, we don't—"

"Shhh. I want you to cum inside me. I need to see your face this time. Please do it. I just want to make you happy."

Menage watched her pull off the jersey and
he began touching her soft skin. He was about
to please her with oral sex, but she forced
him to put the condom on as she guided him
inside her.

"Ooh, Menage," she moaned as he entered
her. "Make it good. Make love to me. Tell me
I'm special when you cum. Please, oh, yes, baby,
yes." She continued to moan as his strokes filled
her with pleasure. Her nails dug into his waist
as he pleased her. Her legs were locked around
his lower back as they kissed and moaned out
to one another. When she noticed him reaching
his climax, she held his face in her hands looked
into his eyes. "Cum, baby, I want it, please cum,"
she said rolling her hips to the rhythm of his
thrusting penis.

Menage's body became stiff. "Oh, Passion!"
Then with quick, rapid strokes, he came, filling
the condom while still calling out her name. She
held him tightly until he finished. Still more
willing to give pleasure than receive it, Menage
licked her entire sweat soaked body from head
to toe and held her in his arms as she cried
herself to sleep. A few hours later when he got
up to use the bathroom and returned to the bed,
he was surprised to find Passion wide awake.

"You okay?" he asked letting her curl up next
to his naked body under the sheets. She felt

warm and soft, and the smell of her sex was deep in his chest. She moved her nails over his chest and spoke in a low, steady voice.

"Menage, we need to talk about what we did."

"Did what?" he asked sliding his hand over her wide bare hips.

"The unprotected sex we had."

He didn't answer as reality hit him. He had only known this woman for a few hours and yet he had unprotected sex with her.

"I don't have any STDs, if that's what you're thinking," said Passion.

"Too late if I was, huh?"

"We both got caught up, I guess. And no, I don't do things like this, so—"

"Passion, wait," he said now laying on his side. "You don't have to explain nothin' to me. We can't change the past, right?" He couldn't see her face in the dim light, but he knew he had put her at ease.

"So we both agree that it was a mistake then?" she asked and gently pushed him onto his back. Menage was silent. He knew she wanted to be wanted and he cut off her next sentence by sliding his tongue through her parted lips. She rolled onto her back, clasped her hands around the back of his neck, and returned the kiss. She felt him growing hard between her parted thighs. She caressed his hard body and moaned as his

mouth left hers and moved to her neck. His
hot breath and wet tongue caused her back to
arch.

"Menage," she cried, as his mouth found her
full breasts. Lower he went, placing wet kisses
on her body. Passion gripped the headboard as
Menage settled his face between her thighs.

"This is no mistake," he said.

Friday

Passion was gone, and Menage now lay in
his backyard by the pool with Vapor at his side,
smoking a blunt as the sun beamed down on
him. He was shirtless, clad only in a pair of baggy
cargo shorts sagging off his waist. He slid his
shades down to block the sun. "Just you and me,
boy," he said stroking Vapor's neck. Menage's
mind wandered back to Chandra. Shit, she
wasn't even his first love. Keama was really the
one who got away . . . Keama . . . but that was
another time and life. He laughed at how he felt
a touch of jealousy when Passion mentioned
her woman friend. So what she went both ways?
There were preachers who were gay, and that
made no damn sense. What, they have a new
bible now? He knew he couldn't pass judgment

since he was fucking everything that moved. He missed Chandra deeply, but he had to get over her and move on. "It's better like this," he said, trying to convince himself that he was content with being alone. The atmosphere was quiet, and the only sounds that could be heard were the wind rustling the leaves of the palm tree over his head and Vapor's heavy panting. Pulling deeply on the blunt to finish it, he slowly stood up from the pool chair. He called Tony at the chop shop and told him he'd be in later. Due to the heat, he pulled off in his topless Acura Legend and wondered if he would feel different once he reached a million.

As soon as Menage closed the door of his car, Tony walked out of the shop, wiping his oily hands on his stained pants. "Thank God you're back, boss," he said in his strong Italian accent as the two walked side by side into MD Body Works. He was Menage's most trusted employee.

"So what's ready to be moved today, Tony?" Menage asked taking his seat behind his desk. Tony told him of cars and SUVs that were tagged and ready to be sold: A Mercury Marauder, a Lexus GX-470, an Audi *AB* 4.2 Quattro, two Lincoln Navigators and a Jaguar

XKR that was worth ninety-five grand. But he'd
let it go for fifty thousand in cash. It didn't take
long for Menage to make a few calls and speak
in code. In less than ten minutes, he had the
XKR sold. Now he was only a hundred grand
away from his goal. Before thirty minutes had
passed, he sold the remaining vehicles in one
shot to a dealership in Gainesville, bringing
him over $175,000 in cash. He hung up the
phone and sat alone in his office, resting his
chin in his hand. He sure as hell didn't feel any
different when he hit the million-dollar mark,
not to mention the dough he had coming from
Dwight. He watched Tony and the rest of the
crew as they removed the windshield from a
midnight black Saab 9-3. That would bring him
another ten thousand. Maybe he'd let Tony
and the crew split it. Even though they were all
treated and paid well, they didn't buy things
that were beyond their earnings.

Menage and Tony had a long talk about
how DJ ran the shop while he was away. He
kept his cool when Tony, who generally didn't
like DJ, broke the news about coke being
placed in a few of the cars that were shipped.
Sure, he broke his own rules by moving the
amount of cars he did today, but those were
his rules, rules that were supposed to be
followed whether he was in a coma or not,

Menage reasoned as he listened to Tony. So, DJ had Xerox and AJ tag the DB-7 and was running coke. And while he was in a coma, Dwight had changed the game. But damn, he couldn't trip; DJ saved his life and Dwight was like a brother. Either way, he knew DJ wouldn't enjoy his phone call. He really hadn't even thanked him for saving his life. But still, that was then and this was now. What really got under his skin was Tony telling him how DJ had tried to act like him and talk like him. He said it seemed that if given the chance, DJ wouldn't have minded changing his name to Menage. First it was the Escalade EXT and then the platinum Vette, the same color as his Benz, Tony pointed out.

Before leaving, Menage still hadn't made up his mind on what path he'd take in dealing with DJ. He didn't even notice the picture of he and Chandra missing from his desk. That was a good thing for DJ.

Lydia pulled into the parking lot of the chop shop. She didn't see the Yellow Escalade, and thought that maybe Menage would be in later. However, she had a reason to be there. Backing into a pole on purpose had left a dent on the back bumper of the RX-330. She knew Myers was strict on how government money was spent.

Tough! She had a job to do. Walking into the shop, she stopped at the door when a topless car spun out and merged into the traffic. "Crazy," she said to herself, not realizing that was Menage, and went inside the shop. Tony met her at the counter with a smile.

"How may I help you?" Lydia told him about the dented bumper. She asked about Menage and Tony told her that she was out of luck and that she had just missed him. She went on to tell him they'd met at a club a while back. Tony noticed what a stunning black beauty she was and he knew his boss was a big flirt, so he couldn't see him letting her off so easy. He found it odd that she didn't have his number; Menage would have made sure a woman this beautiful never lost touch with him. Lydia's car was given immediate attention, and Tony called Menage as she observed the shop from the waiting area.

Menage was cruising down Twenty-seventh Avenue while talking on the phone to a new chick named Shadequa when his phone beeped, letting him know he had another call. Tony quickly told him what was up. Menage didn't hesitate to tell Tony to give the beautiful stranger his number, and switched back to Shadequa.

He'd been trying his hardest to get with her, but she had told him she had a boyfriend and wanted to do right by right him. *Life goes on,* Menage thought. He called Dwight at the salon and told him he was stopping by. As soon as he stepped into the salon, Tylisha spotted him and ran to meet him at the door, leaving her client lying back with her head in the sink. He saw that she was still looking good, a little thicker in the hips, but that was all good. He had slept with her twice, and she was so happy to see him that in no time at all they were making plans for the third round. He gave Jamal dap at the top of the stairway that led down to the barbershop. He tapped twice on Dwight's office door and walked in to find his man on the phone. Dwight motioned for him to come in and take a seat, and as he talked on the phone he got up and went to his safe, taking out the cash he had for Menage. He laid thirty thousand dollars on his desk all in big faccs. Menage looked at the dough and thought about all the drama he would bring up about what DJ had done with the shop, as well as the coke and the DB-7. *Does Dwight have something on the low with DJ? Does he know what was going down? Fuck it*. He decided to just take his spot back and roll with it for now. He looked at the picture on the desk of

Dwight and Tina. Deep down he'd wished he had someone like Tina. Well, not exactly like her, but Dwight really had it made, all the way to his black queen. Dwight hung up the phone and dropped down into his seat with a smile.

"Hey, man, we made it to our dream. Hell yeah!" Menage looked at Dwight and remained silent. He was lost for words and he fought hard not to mention all the things Tony had told him. "You okay, man?" Dwight asked. He thought that maybe Menage was thinking about Chandra.

"It's nothin', man. It's just that I was up all damn night sexin' this chick, only for her to roll out with her Aggressive!"

"*Aggressive?* Who or what is that?"

"Man, you need to get out more. Anyway, it's the same as a lesbian, but they go after feminine girls, and this chick I had was all that. It ain't no big deal!" he lied. His pride really did take a beating the night before. Fortunately, the story came in handy, as he needed to think fast to throw Dwight off from what was really troubling him.

"Damn. Everything straight with the party?" asked Dwight, deciding not to touch the subject any further. Dwight had his full attention now. They agreed to have a million-dollar pool party at Menage's mansion. It would all go down the next day. Big Chubb would provide a healthy supply of fine, black exotic dancers. And all the members from the car club and employees from the salons would be there. The party would start at two and end at midnight, then continue on at Club Limelight before bringing it back to the crib until about four or five in the morning. Menage smiled. He was back in the center of the mix. He was now worth nearly two million dollars, which included his throwaway money and what he had in the bank.

Only a few people would know what the party was really for—Dwight, Tina, and Tony. Everyone else would think that it was just a welcome home party for Menage. He joked with Dwight about Tina having him on lock and how he could only look but not touch. He knew Dwight had work to do, so he took his money out of the briefcase Dwight handed him and left.

He ran into Tylisha outside as she sat on her pink chromed out Honda CBR 600. She made sure they were still set up for later on. "Believe dat!" he said smacking her ass as he headed to his Acura.

Dwight had his secretary call most of MD Beauty Salon VIP customers and invite them to the pool party. Lydia also received a phone call and when the secretary didn't get her directly, she left a message on her answering machine.

Jay-Z's "Hard Knock Life" thundered from the Acura Legend as it cruised down the street. Goosebumps exploded all over Menage's body as he thought about where his life was heading . . . a young-ass nigga with no stress. What more could he ask for? "Yes!" he yelled out, making a fist with his right hand. Ain't nobody been through the shit he'd been through. If they had, then more power to them. But whatever the case, Menage Unique Legend wouldn't let anyone into his heart again. Day by day he would get stronger and just live his life, keep things simple. As he neared his mansion, Dough-Low called and told him that he would be back some time that night and that he'd made a lick. He hit a super lab, and by luck, which Menage didn't believe, he caught his victims about to make a shipment of three kilos of Methamphetamine that was worth three hundred grand.

"Oh, it's true!" Dough-Low said before ending the call. If Dough-Low was telling the truth, then his whole team was making moves. And Menage had to admit that even he was past doin' the damn thang himself. In his eyes, he put the 'ling' in 'bling' the 'pro' in 'filing' and . . . well, some other crazy slogan.

The party tomorrow would be his coming out. He wasn't even going out tonight, and he hoped Tylisha would be up for a long night of sex. As he recalled their last round, he was sure that she would be. There was something about a girl that could pop the clutch on a 600 and bring the front end up with ease. Just before reaching home, he stopped at three different stores and the post office. He wrote out money orders to his mom, nephew, and sister, who was living in Texas. They didn't see each other much, but the love was still there, no doubt.

Vapor was in a playful mood when Menage walked into the mansion, running from room to room, barking at nothing. Menage just smiled and ignored his crazy dog.

Latosha was about to call Menage when she got home after coming up with a good lie, but first she checked her calls. She was convinced that luck was on her side when she got the message about the house party at Menage's place. She knew she had to look good and be the sexiest chick there in order to catch his eye and find out about the DB-7. So far she had gotten nowhere. The CIA didn't let the FBI release any info on Menage and all that went down that night, so it was as if the case never happened. As for Dwight, she had no proof of any criminal activity and she doubted that he had anything to do with the murder, plus he was in Miami when it happened. She tried not to think of the night they had sex, although she had to admit that it was almost too good.

Lydia was aware that Menage was living a lavish life, and she would need to step up her game on material things in order to catch his attention. A blood red Maserati Spyder would be delivered directly to her from the FBI later on today and left in the driveway. *Now that would be nice,* she thought to herself. She'd get to know Mr. Legend, to a point, she told herself. If he spoke on her ride, she'd say something like, "I wish I had one of those James Bond cars," which were mainly Aston Martins. She hoped this statement would cause him to try to impress her and talk about the DB-7. It was a long shot, but it just might work. Men love to brag!

Tina was sitting in her office, singing and snapping her fingers to a cut by Mary J. Blige. Life was good. Her man was sitting on a million, and she now had close to $150,000 in her stash. She even had another new whip, an Onyx Lexus

SC-430. And finally her man would have a car that would top Menage's S600. The gold Bentley Continental GT would show up just in time for the party. All eyes would be on them when they pulled up in the Bentley Coup. Millionaires do big things! Yes, life was good for Tina, and the engagement ring on her finger had her on cloud nine. Things were was so good that she even laid off from her little sex games behind Dwight's back. Some niggas were just so damn blind! But she had to give it to Menage. He was one smooth muthafucka!

"Solo, can you get the phone for me, baby?" Benita yelled from the shower. Solo was slumped back on the couch in the living room with his hand in his pants. He wanted to join Benita in the shower so damn bad, but she told him she didn't rush into things like that. For three weeks they'd been together, and the farthest he got was sucking on her tits. But she was worth the wait, and he'd play the waiting game with her. When she told him that she was a stripper, he thought it would be instant motel action. Wrong! And off the top she told him she wasn't getting involved with any drug dealer or anybody with baby mama drama. Fortunately, for Solo, he was neither. At twenty-seven, he had his own apartment in Carol City and a tight forest green Toyota Foreunner. He really wished he had the money to cop some dubs, but Benita didn't stress all that flashy stuff. She was satisfied that he had a job at the airport.

"Who was it?" she asked, stepping out of the bathroom wearing a long towel.

"Uh, some lady just invited you to a pool party happenin' tomorrow. I got the address. You goin'?" he asked looking her over.

"Do *you* wanna go?"

"Yeah, why not?" He pictured her in a two-piece, then nothing at all.

"Who's it for?"

"Something for all the people that go to some salon . . . MD Salon."

"Oh," she said, then stepped back into the bathroom. They were alone since Lisa was out with DJ. Making sure the bathroom door was shut, he reached into this pocket and pulled out the small bottle of date rape pills. He was tired of waiting and he wondered if they would really work. He continued to contemplate while she got dressed.

"Dang, it's hot out here," Benita said walking to her Ocean Blue Chrysler Crossfire. "I'll call you when I'm on my way back home. You coming back over, right?" she asked getting into her car.

"Yeah, if you gonna give me some of that ass," Solo wanted to say. But instead he said, "Yeah, just page me if I'm not home. I'll swing back by." He closed the door for her and walked toward his truck.

"Okay, boo," she said leaning out the window to give him a wet kiss. Pulling out from behind Solo's Forerunner, she honked her horn at him and headed to the mall to buy a new bathing suit for the pool party. *Maybe Menage will be there,* she thought as she cruised down Twenty-ninth Avenue, singing along with a tune by Monica and tapping the steering wheel.

Menage made a left turn on Sixty-second Street while banging Field Mob in his S600.

"What's this?" Tylisha yelled, holding up a small digital tape she found in the armrest.

"Gimme that." Menage snatched it from her, tossing it onto the backseat. She sucked her teeth.

"Knowing you, it's a damn porno flick," she said squinting from the blazing sun beaming through the open sunroof. She glanced out of the dark tinted windows. Even with the AC on it was still hot. She smiled slyly and took off her shirt. Menage was pleased when he saw her full tits. "It's so hot," she said, leaning back in the seat, wrapping her arms around the headrest. "My ta-tas need some air." She closed her eyes and sighed.

In no time they were back at Menage's mansion. Still topless, Tylisha fell back onto his bed as he buried his face between her breasts. Unfastening her jeans, she lifted up to slide them down her long legs. Kneeling on his knees, Menage massaged her breasts and Tylisha pulled down his jeans and boxers. He stopped and removed his shirt. Menage was the only guy Tylisha knew who would satisfy her needs, even when it came to a quickie, and everything about him excited her. She loved to see the sweat form over his body, the faces he would make when he slid into her, the way he called out her name. She could go on, but right now she focused on sucking him. He made slurping noises between her parted thighs, as they pleased each other in the sixty-nine position with her on top. When he told her to put the condom on him, she found herself wanting him inside of her with nothing between them. She wanted to be his girl. She knew she wasn't bad looking, she had no kids, and she even had the chance to be one of Luke's dancers. *Why wouldn't he want me*? She continued sucking him, trying to make it the best head he'd ever had. Tylisha had heard the older ladies say that the way to a man's heart is through his stomach. Well, she'd just have to take her chances with his dick in her mouth or any other place he wanted to put it. After putting the condom on Menage, she rode him, balancing herself on the balls of her feet, hands braced on his chest. She wondered if she would be this open if he was broke and worked at Footlocker or some other bullshit place. *Nah, but damn if the sex ain't bangin',* she thought as she continued to rock on top of him, giving it all she had.

"Mmm, 'Nage, you so good to me, baby!" she said, breathing heavily as her tits flopped around along with the rhythm of her bucking motion. Never pulling out, he rolled her over and secured her thighs with his arms. He slammed into her, causing her eyes to roll toward the back of her head. If she ever did become his girl, she made up her mind to get this dick as much as possible. Her hands slid down his back, then back up, sending a chill all the way to his toes.

"I-missed-you-baby," she panted. "Please don't stop doing this to me!" she shouted. She blurted it out so fast that he couldn't make out

what she had said. It didn't matter to him; he
knew it was just lust that had her caught up. *To
hell with nutting in a condom,* Tylisha thought.
In her mind she had to prove to him that she
was special, and that would definitely do it.
She quickly made him stand up beside the bed.
Dropping to her knees, she took his throbbing
penis back into her mouth and slowly slid her
glossy lips over it. She rubbed it all over her face
and talked to it while appearing to be in a daze.
Menage entered her mouth again, and he threw
his head back and dropped his jaw. She moaned
and fondled his sac. Then she worked faster and
grabbed his tight ass.

"Ooh, shit, Tylisha!" he said looking down at
her lips moving steadily on his penis. He could
feel her tongue going around and around on
his head and he squeezed the base of his penis
to keep from cumming. Tylisha was going so
fast that her mouth was making a wet, popping
sound as she took him deeper and deeper. She
wanted him so badly that tears began to run
down her face. She felt no shame. Menage never
came in her mouth before, and he did the best
he could to indicate that he was close to that
point. She continued to suck steadily. "Tylisha!"
he yelled. She palmed his ass even tighter now
to keep him from getting away from her hungry

mouth. Menage got up onto his tiptoes, having to reach for the wall to keep from falling as he spurted a full load into her mouth. Seconds later he was on his back with his eyes closed, trying to catch his breath as Tylisha purred and caused him to twitch by gently lapping the juices from his penis. For the first time she presented a challenge to him in the bedroom.

"I did that because I really care about you," she said. It didn't take long for Menage to strap up and mount her again. This time he had her in the doggie style position on the floor while reaching between her legs and stimulating her clit. She cursed him when the first spasms exploded in her body as he continued to drive into her. They took a shower afterward and she again gave him oral sex. Riding down the elevator she latched onto his arm, eyes and heart full of lust. She hoped, as he took her back home, that she'd be on his mind a lot more after this last scenario. Before he drove off, she kissed him deeply and told him to call her soon, real soon. Menage said he would, but by the time he reached the end of her block he had forgotten all about her. "CD six, song two, volume max," he said cracking all the windows down halfway. Activating the system on his spinning rims, he pushed the big S600 with one hand on the steering wheel, leaning to the side, while Eightball & MJG's "Pimp Hard" blared so loudly that he felt the thumping bass vibrate deep in his chest. He wore orange Nike cotton jogging pants, an XXL white Nike T-shirt, and a pair of custom made orange and white Nikes. His Bulova and platinum chain shined in the beaming sun. Goosebumps popped up all over his body as he cruised through a busy inter-section in Hialeah. This was Dade County, and it was no surprise to Menage that he had six new phone numbers from chicks who had flagged him down. Then there was the one he had to make a U-turn for after seeing her at a bus stop. She was voluptuous in all the right places.

Menage pulled up to Li'l Coonk's crib. He saw that the street was already filled with flashy whips. He parked behind a midnight Lincoln Aviator sitting on 23s. Menage walked inside the house and felt as though he had entered a small casino. He made his way into the kitchen to find a table loaded with cash, beer bottles, and lit blunts. Seven Cards was the game. There were five players seated at the table, including Li'l Coonk, and Menage knew everyone: Otis, Drelex, Deck, and Lou, and he knew the stakes were high. Li'l Coonk's baby's mama was making sure the beer kept moving, and every step she made, a red nosed pit bull followed. Menage noticed a sexy white chick checking him out from behind a pair of blue tinted Christian Dior sunglasses. She was average looking, sporting skintight black velour pants by Fendi, and a matching front zipper halter top. She was about five feet ten inches with a firm body and large full breasts.

Li'l Coonk pointed to an empty chair. "Grab a seat. I'm taking all the money. Tamica, grab 'Nage a brew," he yelled over the loud music.

"Yeah, deal me in, Dre, so I can't send all y'all to the stash. Coonk done called me out." Drelex shuffled the cards and the white chick walked over and stood behind Menage.

"You don't mind, do ya?" she asked.

"Nah, you straight," he said over his shoulder.

Coonk caught Menage's eye and then looked at the girl standing behind him. "Jungle fever," he quickly mouthed looking back at Menage. Menage just smiled, and he noticed that the fourth card he was dealt was another Ace . . . four of a kind. He looked around the table.

"Aces high, nigga!" Coonk said.

"Bet twenty," Menage said. Everybody stayed. His fifth card was a three of hearts. He looked at the other five hands on the table. Drelex, who was a new member, had nothing showing. Otis was next to him, squinting his eyes from the Newport in his mouth. He peered from under his hoodie. He had two Kings and a Jack was up. Coonk took a pull from the blunt he was smok- ing. "Aces still high, nigga!" Three hearts were up. Lou sat back in the chair and looked at the white girl. He was working on a straight. Deck sat on Menage's right, his long dreads covering his face. He didn't have shit.

"Bet twenty," Menage said milking the whole table. Lou wanted to show off in front of the sexy white chick. "Yo, I raise you. Aces leave you lonely. Bet sixty." Nobody wanted to look weak in front of the white chick, and they all called.

Menage was still high so he turned up the gas. He tried to be nice, but niggas wanted to play hardball. He reached into his pocket and pulled out a knot. With his elbows on the table, he counted out five hundred dollars and tossed it in the pile of cash that was already in the middle of the table. Everybody called. Lou started to raise, but he didn't. $3,480 was in the pot. The last card was turned face down. With a straight face, Menage bet two hundred in the dark with the option to raise. Drelex, Otis, and Coonk folded their hands.

Lou glanced at Deck to see if he was going to call the two hundred. "Menage, I know all you got is Aces over there," he said grilling Menage.

"Call the bet den, and quit talkin' me ta deaf." Menage knew he couldn't touch Lou as far as money was concerned.

"Yeah, I'ma call that shit," Lou said pulling out a knot of crisp hundred-dollar bills. "Plus, I'ma raise you five hundred," he added. He counted out the bills slowly.

"Shit, that's seven hundred to you, Deck," Li'l Coonk said rolling a blunt.

"Damn, Lou!" Deck exclaimed. "What you raise for?"

"Man, fold that shit and quit chasing and catching cards!" Lou said with a smirk.

Menage sat back in his seat and looked at his last card, which he didn't need. He knew that if he raised Lou, he would call, and folding was not a word to Lou. Thinking of the sexy white chick behind him, he called the bid and flipped over his four aces—a winner.

"Damn!" Lou yelled, reaching over to look at the four aces with a closer look. Calling it a day, Menage later found himself in the living room, dancing and smoking weed with the white chick as a song by the Notorious B.I.G. played. A few more chicks showed up later and it turned into a house party. He noticed a dark-skinned chick in homemade *Daisy Dukes* and high-heeled clogs, making her taller and sexier. Still with the white chick, whose name was Nicole, Menage made a mental note that there was a difference in her after she went into the bathroom and came out. She had secretly popped a few ecstasy pills. Her top was halfway zipped down now, showing her tanned, creamy cleavage. When she pressed her tits up against him, he smiled and moved her hair out of her face. He easily detected the "I wanna get fucked" look in her eyes.

"So, where your girl at?" she asked placing her arms around his neck, still staying with the beat of the loud music.

"Same place yo' man at," Menage said palming her round ass.

"I've seen you around," she said in his ear, "and I've been wanting to get with you, but it was like, some girl was always on your shoulder and like . . . well, I didn't know if you went the white way."

Menage's head jerked back and he looked into her blue eyes. "The white way!"

"Uh-huh," she said nodding her head. "You should see me in a black garter set."

"Well, dis is how I see it, shorty . . . " he said rubbing her ass even harder. A chick dancing with a bottle of Bull in her hand and a blunt in the other told someone to turn up the radio that was now banging R. Kelly's "Ignition." "Like I was sayin', I be really on the move, so—"

"Let's go to your place and do something kinky, Menage," Nicole said feeling the E kicking in. She slowly tucked in her bottom lip, adding emphasis to her point.

"You got a ride?" he asked squeezing her ass. She nodded yes. "Meet me outside in about ten minutes." Walking into the kitchen, Menage happened to look out the back window and saw Lou with his face buried between a pair of thick thighs hooked over his shoulders. He took a good look at the chick on the table.

"Yo, Coonk, Lou done lost his mind, ain't he?"

"Man, that nigga crazy. Yo, what time the party tomorrow?"

"Oh, yeah . . ." Menage said turning from the sex scene. "Come by early . . . like uh, two."

"You 'bout to smash ol' girl?" Coonk said rubbing his red eyes.

"White chick?"

"Yeah," Coonk said wishing they could run a train on her. "You gonna take her to the mansion?"

"Do Miami got palm trees?" They gave each other dap. "But yo, I'ma holla at cha tomorrow. Let me raise up out dis muthafucka." Menage walked back into the living room and made his way through the crowd. When he got outside he found Nicole standing next to her black Lexus GX-470. "Follow me," he said.

"So how do I look?" Benita asked looking at herself in the mirror. Solo stood behind her with his hands on her bare waist. The time was so right. It was almost too good to be true. All Benita wore was a two-piece Fendi swimsuit that cost him a month's pay. Seeing her seminude body had him fucked up. She was blood raw and he tried his luck.

"Baby, you know you look good." He kissed her gently on the neck and slowly moved his hands down her hips, following her curves down toward her thick thighs. She tilted her head back and let out a deep breath. Solo was running his hands over the thin material of her thong now, and then slowly moved them upward, massaging her stomach.

"Solo," Benita whispered, feeling his mouth work at the clasp on her top. He wanted to drive into her right now, but he knew he had to play it easy. Feeling her bikini top come off, he turned her around and nearly lost his breath at the sight of her juicy tits in his face. He ran his hands over them, lifting them, pressing them together.

"Solo," she moaned, as his tongue circled her nipples. He was past hard and he slowly led her to the bed. Still sucking her breasts, he laid down next to her, running his hand up and down her stomach, stopping at the top of her thong.

"Oh, Benita," he murmured with a mouthful of tit and nipple. He vowed that last night was the last time he'd masturbate with his eyes closed thinking of Benita. He pulled at the string on the side of her hip. She opened her legs and thrust her hips forward when she felt his finger rub against her throbbing clit through the thin thong.

"Solo," she cried feeling his tongue flick over her hard nipple.

"I-I love you so much, Benita," he lied, fumbling with his belt to free himself. Benita's mind was made up. She would do whatever her body told her to.

Nicole was willing to take Menage raw, but he turned her down. He didn't want to take any risks. Still she went all out and tried to freak him like no one ever had before. She used her mouth on him and let him shoot on her face, something she desperately wanted him to do. She allowed him to do her in any position as she moaned out his name over and over, telling him to take it. When she rode him she looked deep into his eyes, hoping to find something that she knew would never exist. It was so good to her that she grabbed her head with both hands, calling out his name as he drove into her hard and fast. "Oh, Menage!"

Chapter 3

Nuttin' In The Dark

Late Saturday Night
11:28 p.m.

The million-dollar party was wide open at Menage's mansion. The backyard was packed with close to two hundred heads. Every member of the Big League was on hand. The five strobe lights and the glowing pool caused a few to strip and take a swim. Big Chubb had a group of his top dancers dancing near the pool to make a few dollars. Dough-Low was behind the turntable spinning records and hyping up the crowd with Biz Markie's "Nobody Beats The Biz." Li'l Coonk was inside spiking the punch with a bottle of Hypnotiq and Gin. Tina and Dwight were having a good time. She was Prada down and dropping it like it was hot, and she even allowed Dwight to spark an L. Dwight was dapper in his custom made, denim Kevlar Silvertab jeans and jacket.

Lisa and DJ were amongst the crowd, dancing and getting their drink on. They both sported gear by Pelle Pelle. To keep a nigga in check, just in case, Dough-Low had two nickel-plated 45s tucked under his armpits.

The air was perfect, and there was a cool breeze coming from the sea that made the palm trees in the backyard sway back and forth. Benita was inside the stunning mansion sipping the drink that Solo had just given her. She was a little upset that he had picked her up so late, and she had come close to driving herself to the party.

"Thank you for the drink," she said looking at the large eighty-inch TV screen and then at the elevator.

"I said I'm sorry, Benita," said Solo in his most pitiful sounding voice. Benita sucked her teeth and told him to sit down. *Dang, Dwight has a fly crib,* she thought as Solo slid closer to her. Solo knew he was out of his league when he parked next to a yellow Lotus Esprit Turbo. Maybe some baller would snatch Benita right from under his nose. And he couldn't believe how it was going down, chicks walking around wearing string bikinis. One blood raw chick ran through the living room topless, and some lucky guy was chasing her.

"Hey, boo, let's go out back and dance. I think I see my silly tail cousin anyway," Benita said after finishing her drink, which she told herself would be her only one. She quickly scanned the scene for Menage. The thought of him made her pull Solo closer to her, placing his hands on her waist as she danced with her back to him. Solo wasn't balling, but he sure as hell had the baddest chick. He thought for sure he was going to fuck her yesterday, but it was all good because he knew she would be more than willing after those two pills kicked in that he'd slipped in her drink. He wondered if she would move the same way later once he got her on her back. He made up his mind to go raw. His thoughts were interrupted when Dough-Low started to show his mixing skills. Everyone yelled "Oat's da shit!" when he began playing a cut by Das EFX.

Lydia made looking beautiful and sexy as easy as breathing. She held a glass of Hennessey and snapped her fingers as she danced with Jamal, Dwight's head barber. By using FBI funds to play the part, she sported killer Louis Vuitton skin-tight jeans with matching sandals that wrapped around her calves. She wore a thin black mesh halter-top. Jamal couldn't believe he was dancing with her. Lydia didn't realize that Jamal was falling for her because she was too busy scanning the crowd for Menage. She didn't really want to dance, but being a wallflower would have made her stick out. *If this is Menage's mansion, then his beauty salon and body shop are doing damn good,* she thought to herself. As for Dwight, he ignored her, not that she gave a damn. And she couldn't lie and say she wasn't having a ball, as she slowly rotated her firm stomach with her drink waving in the air.

A few of Big Chubb's strippers started making money when Akinyele's "Put It In Your Mouth" sent the crowd into a zone. And it was no surprise when some of them got naked. Lydia shook her head when a group of guys surrounded two of the strippers on the hood of a stunning peach Jaguar XKR. They were in the sixty-nine position, giving each other oral sex. The backyard, at the same time, was close to turning into a mini freaknik.

Lydia had told Jamal that she needed to use the bathroom, which was a lie. She didn't want any distractions right now. But Jamal forgot all about her when he bumped into one of his coworkers.

Tina was feeling horny, and she led Dwight inside the mansion. She knew Dwight had the code to get into one of the rooms, and she knew her man would tend to her needs as soon as the door was shut.

Dough-Low was still on the turntables as the crowd sung along to a hit by Keith Murray. He was hitting them with the hot shit. "We . . . do dis like . . . we want to and don't give a fuck!" everyone chanted with their hands in the air as the five strobe lights started flashing on top of the thumping speakers.

Lydia checked out the scene. She reminded herself to not get another drink, even though the one she was nursing was very tasty. *Now, where is Menage?* she thought as she looked around. She flung her hair over her shoulder. *Where is he?* Suddenly, a shot rang out, causing Lydia to nearly drop her glass. The crowd paused for a split second, never missing a beat, before realizing that it wasn't a gunshot. Menage had ridden up on his Suzuki Hayabusa 1300-R and was doing a burnout in the backyard. The loud stutter box was the source of the noise. Behind him, holding onto his waist, was a thick, deep chocolate colored woman with fine twisted locks. She was clad only in a bra and thong. Menage smoked the back tire, and the girl with him ignored someone pulling at the string of her skimpy bra, causing it to come off. Menage came off the clutch, bringing the front end up just as he and his passenger splashed into his pool, bike and all. Menage got out of the pool, soaking wet from head to toe, but he really didn't care because he was high as a kite. Li'l Coonk tried to get him to sit down, but he ignored him and pulled his topless friend out of the pool. He headed toward the music and wondered when Tylisha would show up. *Superhead!*

Solo couldn't believe his eyes; it was like a P. Diddy video. He looked at Menage like he was a fool for destroying a 1300-R like it wasn't shit. Solo glanced at his fake platinum watch and searched the crowd, standing on the tips of his toes. He spotted Lisa dancing in front of DJ. He eased through the crowd, copping a feel on some ass wherever he could.

Lisa snapped her fingers and grinded her ass into DJ as he held on for dear life. Now this was a party, and she couldn't believe that Benita had let Menage slip away; that fool was paid! DJ had told her that MD Beauty Salon was owned by Menage and Dwight. Lisa couldn't help but sneak a peek at Menage. Even high, he was still sexy as hell, dancing with some slut and having the balls to be sucking on her nipple. *Damn, he's bold,* Lisa thought. *Well, at least Benita's over him. He ain't nothing but a dog anyway. Solo's not paid, but he's a nice guy.* Just as Lisa refocused her attention on DJ, Solo made his way through the crowd, nodded toward DJ and yelled in Lisa's ear.

"Yo, you seen Benita?"

"Nah, she might be inside. Something wrong?"

"Nah, just lost her. I' ll check inside then." Turning around, he walked back through the wild crowd. Looking at his watch again, he knew the date rape pills he put into Benita's drink were taking effect, but where in the helI was she? Solo was so horny that he made up his mind to do her at this mansion. He smiled and quickly started his search for the more than willing Benita.

Menage stumbled into his dark bedroom. He tripped on a pair of shoes or slippers . . . hell, he didn't know what it was but he crawled the last few feet to his toilet and called earl. The Moet, Heineken, and Armadale Vodka mix drink that Li'l Coonk had given him had made his stomach turn inside out. He reached up and grabbed the tube of Crest toothpaste, flipped the top and squeezed a large amount into his rank, foul-smelling mouth. His head still spinning, he staggered out of the bathroom . . . just ten steps and he'd make it to his bed. He didn't notice that his bedroom door was closed now. He could still hear the loud music out back and Dough-Low yelling into the mic for the girls to get topless. He paid it no mind. All he cared about was getting in his bed. Stepping out of his damp jeans, he stripped naked and stumbled into his bed. He laid on his back, wearing only his platinum name piece medallion. Just as he closed his eyes, he felt a hand reach between his legs. He slurred something and reached out in the dark, placing his hands on a soft pair of legs. Lust took over as he moved his hands between the already-parted thighs. The body was naked and wet. Rolling over, he hooked the legs in the crook of his arms and placed his chain around the woman's neck. He was above her on his knees, head still spinning, but his body acted on its own. He French kissed the chick as he felt her guide him inside her. Menage grunted and fell on top of her, moving into her sex. She was tight, awfully tight! They thrashed about on the bed for six or seven minutes before Menage was deep inside her. He passed out on his last jerk.

The party was coming to an end, and now it was time to take it to Club Limelight. Solo had given up on his search for Benita, but he managed to bag a Foxy Brown look-a-like. She was just a little thicker and willing without any pills. *Benita could walk home. Silly chick.*

DJ sat alone in his new blue Jaguar S Type R. Lisa had left early said something had come up with Benita. Oh, well, he still planned to hit the club. He slid up the black tinted window and popped in a Mobb Deep CD. He looked on with envy as Dwight opened the passenger's door of his Gold two-door Bentley for Tina. *But of course, twenties are under the wheel well.* "Stupid ass-nigga!" he said popping the collar on his camel skin Sean Jean Jacket.

Menage was stepping out of the shower as Dough-Low stood by his bed. "Nigga, how da hell you knock some chick off and don't know who it was? I thought you was hit up when I hit the lights. Blood all on the sheets. Either she was a virgin or her period was on."

Menage went to his closet and grabbed the closest thing on the rack, a black lambskin lightweight jacket by Armani. "Man, I don't remember nothin'. Let's bounce. I'ma ride wit' you."

Menage was up in VIP at Club Limelight, overlooking the huge mirrored dance floor as it rotated. The crowd was moving to the thumping beats of Goodie Mob. For once Menage sat alone on the sideline. He smiled when he saw Dwight and Tina on the dance floor. Tina was looking fine as hell, wearing a pair of tight low rider jeans and a top with her belly exposed. The glass of Dom Perignon sat untouched on the table before Menage. He rested his chin in the palm of his hand as the strobe lights flashed off and on to the beat. Maybe there was more to life than cars and chicks. He knew the women were using him just as he was using them. Sure, he was good for sex, but sex didn't make a man, he realized. Every time these thoughts crossed his mind, he would envy the tight relationship Dwight had with Tina. Deep down, if given the chance, he knew he would trade it all in for true love. Dwight had told him over and over to be true to Chandra. But no, he wanted to be a player.

Menage's watch read 4:58 a.m. He got up and walked down the stairs. Lil Jon's "Get Low" had the club fully cranked up now.

Lydia had watched Menage get up and head for the steps. If she hurried, she could catch up to him before losing him in the crowd. She quickly adjusted her top to expose more cleavage. Her leather capri pants fit her like a second skin, and the pumps she wore made her look stunning. Maybe, just maybe she would finally meet him, if some female weren't already up in his face as usual. But after eyeing him all night, she understood totally.

Menage moved through the crowd with ease, ignoring the "Hey cuties" and "What's up niggas." He gave no one eye contact as he approached the door. By the time he made it outside, he realized that he hadn't driven. *Damn!* Knowing Dough-Low, he'd be the last one to come out of the club. He let out a deep breath and looked up at the sky. Fuck it. He'd just call a cab. His phone chimed before he could call a car service.

"Yeah!" he answered, pinching the bridge of his nose.

"May I speak to Menage?"

"Speak. Who dis?" he asked not recognizing the sexy voice.

His head was still hurting.

"Latosha."

"I don't know no Latosha," he said thinking of how she could've gotten his number or stolen it from some chick who ran her mouth too much. And Menage was certain that whoever this Latosha was, she wanted to see if what she had heard about him was true.

"Well, maybe you can change that in due time."

"Look, I'ma have to call you back. I gotta call a cab, okay?"

"Get real."

"Yeah, it's real. I'm broke with no whip. You still wanna holla?" He never heard her reply before ending the call. As he was calling a cab, a red Maserati pulled up next to him with its top down. He couldn't help but to stare at the beautiful black woman behind the wheel who strongly resembled Tweet.

"So that's how we are gonna start out, with you hanging up in my face? And to answer your question, yes, I still wanna holla," Lydia said grinning. Menage smiled. She was smooth, and she had a nice whip. He wondered what she really knew about him.

"Hey, didn't you come by my shop the other day and holla at my man, Tony?"

"Yes, but are we gonna talk like this or can I give you a lift home?"

"What's the cost?" he asked, his chin tilted upward.

"Conversation," she replied softly, flinging her silky hair over her shoulder.

"Deal," he said as he got into the sporty car. And damn if she couldn't handle it, spinning out of the parking lot like Jeff Gordon coming out of pit lane.

***

Menage was silent the entire ride home. Tylisha, the white chick, the stripper at the party, and the unknown girl in his bedroom . . . four in two days could drain a nigga, but he'd be all over the woman sitting next to him if it hadn't been such a fucked up day. It was after five now. He knew she was out for a booty call and if he didn't put out, his name would be dirt. *Should've called that damn cab.* He quickly eyed Lydia. She was sexy as hell. He knew he'd have no problem getting it up. Actually it already was. He smiled to himself. There was some thing classy about her, and she was shaped like Chandra!

"Your man let you stay out this late?" he asked as she pulled up to his gate.

"See any rings on my fingers?" she asked drumming them on the steering wheel. The gate slowly opened as Menage pointed a small device at its sensors.

"So how much?" he asked reaching into his pocket, playing her game. He'd put it all on her.

"Conversation, like I said." The sleek car moved forward past the gate.

"At five in the morning?" he asked glancing at his Bulova. Lydia brought the car to a stop and looked straight ahead, her arms bracing the steering wheel. She knew what would happen if she went into this man's house. *But will he open up to me? Is it that important to get info on the DB-7 and find out who killed the Mayor's son?* Lydia started to wonder how in the hell she got herself in this position. It would be love to be living like he was or be his girl, but here she was undercover trying to lock his ass up.

"Hey, you okay?" he asked breaking her train of thought. "We can get up tomorrow. Trust me. I ain't going nowhere," he said checking her out. *Damn, she's sexy . . . really sexy.*

Lydia nervously turned off the car and looked at Menage. She had a job to do. He was caught off guard when she leaned over, placed her small hand behind his head and kissed him deeply. He responded by leaning toward her and placing his hand on her thigh. It wasn't romance-heart stopping, stars and all that bull-shit. He was simply rock hard. And it wouldn't be the first time he'd have sex with a woman on their first day of meeting, even though Lydia didn't in any way look desperate for a man. But none of that mattered to Menage.

Menage felt like he was in one of those Doublemint chewing gum TV ads as they kissed on his living room couch. He was on his back in no time, caressing her tits as her hand slowly stroked his penis after she freed it from his jeans. Piece by piece their clothes came off, and after Lydia saw Menage's crystal clear pre-cum peeking through his boxers, she knew he wasn't burning. Sure, she planned to make him use protection, but she might want to do some other things. She came up a few inches and placed her tits in his face as she felt his hands move toward the belt and zipper on her leather pants.

"Suck 'em, baby," she said cradling his head. Menage finally had her down to her panties, rubbing her ass under the silky material. She was so soft. She reminded him of Chandra and he didn't know if that was a good thing or not. She placed hot wet kisses on his chest as she moved downward to pull off his boxers. His masculine body had her wet and ready. They positioned themselves side-by-side on the couch to face each other. Lydia was so wet that his fingers were making gushing sounds. Her hands continued to slowly move up and down. She wanted him now, but she was going to wait.

"Oh God, Menage, please don't do that to me, please," she pleaded as he started eating her. Her legs were wide open and he licked her as if his life depended on it. She begged him not to stop, falling back on her elbows, tits jiggling with the jerking of her hips at his mouth. Then she grabbed a firm hold of her tits and screamed out his name as his tongue shattered her plan of seducing him. Her entire body was trembling when she came. He kept caressing her with his tongue, strongly driven by her natural scent. Breathing heavily, she cried out his name over and over, basking in a sexual daze. He picked her up, tonguing her again, letting her taste herself on his lips. Little did she know this was just the beginning.

Menage gently caressed Lydia's breasts, and arousal swept through her body as they lay in his bed. He was gentle with her and didn't rush anything. She had her mind and body set for a quickie, but he was making love to her. He looked deep into her eyes with each stroke as the blue light enveloped them in the bedroom. He wasn't as big as Dwight, but he still pleased her fully. She shivered as he continued to slide in and out of her, and it seemed that with each stroke she moved further away from her plan of seducing him, not to mention doing her job. She lost control and started to arch her back with each thrust, begging him not to stop. She wrapped her hands around his neck as he drove her crazy with desire.

"Who's is it?" he asked seductively as Maxwell played in the background. She didn't answer, but that soon changed as he added more power to his strokes.

"Who's is it?" he asked again as he felt her legs relax and tighten around his pumping pelvis.

"Don't do this to me. Ah, so good!" she said and bit his shoulder.

"Who's is it?" he asked still stroking with one of her legs now up over his shoulder. She took a deep breath as he went deeper inside of her. He had yet to pick up his speed, but this slow love making was obviously something she couldn't fight. It felt good to them both. Tears of frustration fell from the corners of her eyes. The thought of her seducing him was now a joke. She wanted him to stop, needed him to stop. Her hips rocked as her sex gripped his stroking penis tightly.

"Who's is it?" he asked her again as he lowered his body and began flicking his tongue over her parted lips. She was too stunned to speak. But the first spasms went through her body like a volt. He bit his bottom lip and started to roll his hips rhythmically as she grabbed the back of his neck. Just as he filled the rubber, she cried out that it was his. Exhausted, he fell on top of her and called it a night or morning and rested between her parted legs. They slept naked in each other's arms.

Benita lay in her bed, blinking back the tears that filled her eyes. Why had Solo humiliated her the way he did, have sex with her and leave her bloody and dazed? Lisa had found her just before she had passed out. Seeing her bloody jeans, Lisa thought she was just drunk and on her period. But the truth was that Menage had taken her virginity. She hated herself for getting so drunk and off of one drink at that. She could only recall a few things feeling funny and then getting into that bed and doing things to herself. It all seemed like a dream. Then Solo had rushed into the dark room and got into the bed with her. He seemed drunk, but he didn't drink or smoke. He took her, but yet she was willing, wasn't she? Why did it happen? Benita couldn't recall a lot of things, and she couldn't understand how and why Menage's platinum medallion was sitting on the dresser. Lisa had given Benita her bedroom for the night and she'd sleep on the couch. She was mainly worried about her cousin and not the medallion she had worn. Lisa didn't think twice about how it had gotten there before removing it from around Benita's neck.

Benita was just as lost now as she was when she had first tried to forget about The Legend. "W-why, Solo?" she whispered to herself in the dark room after her cousin left. Benita had to keep this a secret, at least for now, and being drunk and having her period would be her cousin's take on the whole thing. The platinum *Legend* name piece lay on the dresser, covered by some of Benita's clothes as she began to come to her right mind while falling asleep, possibly forgetting the entire incident forever.

Chapter 4

Love's Taken Over: Catchin' Feelings

Sunday Afternoon

Benita sat in her favorite spot on the couch watching *Friday* on a DVD. She needed a good laugh. Lisa was somewhere with DJ again, and she was home alone. A box of glazed dough-nuts sat on her lap and a bottle of Sprite was on the table. Her day started off like shit. She had called Solo and before she could speak, she heard some bitch yell in the background, asking if she could use his toothbrush. *Fuck Solo!* Her room was a mess, and the medallion sat on her dresser under a tank top she had tossed, so she still hadn't seen it. She planned to go see Solo later, but first she had to get herself together after that phone call.

The doorbell rang. She knew it was Solo. She quickly put on her shoes. She was mad as hell and her adrenalin was in over drive when she flung the door open with all her might.

"What the fuck do you want, you sorry motherfucker?" she yelled, ready to slap the shit out of Solo. But as soon as she realized that it wasn't Solo, she gasped. "Oh my God, oh my God!" she said over and over as she slowly backed away from the door.

Menage frowned and then looked behind him before turning back around. "You talkin' to me?" he asked pointing to his chest. He took it upon himself to step inside and close the door as Benita, still in shock, backed up until she fell onto the couch. He took a seat next to her, waiting for her to get herself together. She was still looking good, wearing a pair of cotton gym shorts and a white T-shirt. He couldn't help but look at the thickness of her thighs-mouth-watering.

She didn't know what to do or say. She couldn't be upset because he hadn't called. It wasn't like they were dating . . . but still. *Damn, he looks so good . . . a true fucking legend.*

"W-why didn't you ever call me, boy?"

"Long, long story."

"Be strong," she said to herself. *Dang, he got me trippin'. Relax, girl.* "Boy, I've been driving myself crazy thinking about you. And when I came back from North Carolina I heard you was shot again. Then I couldn't find out shit about you. Even Dwight didn't know anything. Well at least that's what he told me." Menage remained silent. "And come to think of it, you met my cousin, Lisa!"

"Lisa?"

"Yeah, DJ's girl. She's a nurse. She told me 'bout that night she ran into you, and that heifer didn't even call me!"

"Oh, yeah, I remember her now." *Hot-in-the-ass Lisa.*

"So where the hell you been at?"

"Had to leave the country for a few weeks."

"Hmmm, another girl?" She wished she could take that back.

"Nope."

"Seriously, though, I never had the chance to thank you. God, Menage, you saved my life. And then you just vanished into thin air." She hoped he didn't see her last night with Solo. "Did you see me last night?"

"Where? Club Limelight?"

"No, boy! I'm talking about the party last night at Dwight's house."

"Dwight's house?" he asked with surprise in his voice. "You talkin' 'bout the mansion with the pool in the back and the big ass TV in the living room?"

"Yeah, were you there?"

"Girl, that's *my* place. Why did you think it was Dwight's?"

She cocked her head to one side. "For real?" She felt really stupid.

"Yes, for real. I didn't see you there, and I don't know how I could've missed you. But I was truly fucked up. Who were you with?"

"I came by myself," she lied, not knowing why.

"Oh, so what's been up with you?"

"Same old stuff, still in school, and yes, I'm still dancing. What about you?"

"Just thinkin' 'bout you."

"Yeah, right. You'll leave once more and I'll have to wait forever to hear from you again."

"Well, I guess I'll just have to prove you wrong and let my actions speak louder than my words. How 'bout that?"

"I got something better."

"What?"

"Shut up and come over here and give me a hug, boy. I really missed you." Menage embraced her and felt awkward holding her so close. But it sure as hell felt good.

***

"Detective Covington, do you have a second?" asked Mack who worked upstairs in the forensic lab.

"Yeah, come on in," Covington said wishing he had a Newport.

Mack ran his fingers through his dirty blond hair and sat down as he cleared his throat.

"Is Detective Hamilton still on leave?"

"Yeah. Why? What's up?"

"Well, he told me to give the results of the tests I ran only to him for the results of some new prints on the hit or attempt case. I lifted the prints off a recording device that was hidden in the bathroom, and they belong to Menage himself. Hamilton said he's sure the tape was taken after the shooting. But I'm telling you since you're in charge and I'm about to go on vacation, so can you pass the info on to him for me?" Detective Covington promised him that he would and thanked him. So there was a tape, a tape he didn't know about, but why was Menage hiding it from him? He opened his file folder and saw that he had for gotten to mail the pictures to Menage of DJ and Tina. Maybe he needed to see Menage face to face and find out about this tape. His uncle, Felix, now somewhere in the South Pacific near the exotic Fiji Islands on his yacht, still wanted to find out who tried to kill Menage.

Lydia sat on the edge of her bed combing her hair. Someone had called Agent Myers and tipped him off with a solid lead on the case, making it obvious that someone in Miami knew about the DB-7 and the murder. She thought about Menage and how they made love again in the kitchen. She would do whatever it took to make whatever leads the FBI had on him vanish. She wanted to break her cover and come clean while he was inside her, but she feared his rejection. She would have to save him and clear his name without his knowledge. As for how she would explain the chop shop to Myers, she'd have to work on that. And she now knew she had to find out who had a grudge against Menage. So far she was sure that the individual was someone close to him. She thought about Dwight but decided against him, and DJ was out of the question because he was the one who saved Menage's life. She had read the reports that Detective Covington had written, and she did something that he didn't always do, follow up. She knew Menage's lifestyle was money, and after a quick call, she was faxed print-outs of the bank statements belonging to Roderick Hopkins, a.k.a. DJ, and Dwight and Tina dated a week before the Bayside shooting. She smiled at the eight grand withdrawn from Tina's account two weeks before the shooting, followed by the withdrawal of the same amount on the next day from DJ's account. Both times the eight grand was circled. Then she recalled hearing at the salon that Tina was cheating on Dwight.

"Hey, I got that news story on tape. Wanna see it?" Benita said as the credits started to roll. She and Menage had finished watching Friday.

"Nah, not really."

"I'm sorry," she said feeling even stupider than before. She looked at the TV with a blank look on her face. She had been curled up under him for the rest of the movie, and instead of paying attention to the flick she focused on how his laugh sounded and how his hand felt resting on her bare thighs. This man had saved her life, so that had to mean something, didn't it? She wanted to ask him why he had come and what he wanted from her. Sex, *like every damn body else, wanna fuck just 'cause*

I got a fat ass and big tits. She got up and changed the DVD. Menage shook his head at her curvaceous body and bit his bottom lip. Being alone with her was driving him crazy, and he was glad to hear his cell phone ring.

"Yeah."

"Menage, this is Covington. What's going on?"

"Holdin' it down. What's the deal wit' you?" he asked watching Benita bending down.

"Hey, I need to ask you something?"

"Shoot."

"What's on that tape you had under your sink?"

There were a few moments of silence. "Yo, how you know about that?" Menage asked covering up his erection with his shirt.

"I'm a detective, remember?" Menage quickly told him that it was a recording of his front gate and driveway. "So it has DJ shooting the guy!"

"Shit, I guess so; I ain't seen it yet." Right now Benita had his full attention.

"Jesus, man, that may be something. Look, I also have something else I need you to look at, so what time can I come and view that tape?"

Menage watched Benita as she walked into the kitchen. Her soft ass cheeks and the way they jiggled in the loose gym shorts she wore mesmerized him. "I'ma spend some time with a lady friend, so hit me back later on tonight," he wanted to say.

"Promise me you'll let me see that tape, man, 'cause the person or people that tried to kill you are still out there, and I'm still on the case."

"Yeah, I hear ya. You got my word. Matter of fact, we'll watch it together." Menage closed his phone and thought about what Covington had said. Yes, it was true. Whoever tried to kill him was still out there. For that he still wore his vest and carried his Glock-19. And Passion's ex was still out there, but he'd been missing after some of Felix's hit men paid him a little visit.

"Leaving me again?" Benita asked sitting next to him.

"Nope. So what you got planned for today?" he asked pulling her closer to him.

"Nothing really. But I have to pick up my cousin from the train station later on tonight, and I might have to ride his crazy ass all around Miami. It's his first time down."

"You ate already?" he asked as he got to his feet. He actually wouldn't mind eating *her*.

"Yeah, some doughnuts," she said laughing. "Why, you wanna grab something to eat? Menage nodded. "Let me get dressed right quick," Benita said. Menage went outside and waited for her. It was so hot that he wished he had driven his

Acura. The thought of her naked was driving him crazy.

Benita sat next to Menage in the Gucci leather seats as they cruised down Twenty-seventh Avenue. She had to admit that everything about him was smooth. The sun warmed her legs through the open sunroof and the soothing music was just right. She now knew that he was rich and single according to what he had said. But he didn't look like the type to be single from Benita's point of view. She remembered that he had no kids. That can change in a second, she reasoned. As she looked through the tinted glass, she thought of that sorry-ass Solo. She hated what he did to her, but she couldn't deny that it felt good.

"I know you ain't going to eat here!" she said as he parked at Bayside.

"Nope," he said opening the door of the S600 for her.

"Well, where are we going then?" she said getting out and putting on her shades.

"Girl, just come on." He smiled and held out his hand for her. She took it. She had no idea where he was going as he led her down the pier. She didn't know anything about boats, but she knew what looked good, like she did in her blue Fendi skirt.

"Did you rent a boat or something?"

"Girl, please. I don't know the meaning of rent," he said as he stopped at a sleek green speedboat.

Benita stood there confused. "I know this ain't your boat," she said with one hand on her hip and the other pointing at the boat.

"Can you read?" he asked pointing to the stern. He knelt down and untied his boat from the pier. She looked toward where he had pointed and read *Menage's Way*. "There's a place down in The Keys that you can only get to by water," he said helping her into the boat.

"I've never been on a boat before," she said, not knowing where to sit.

Menage adjusted her seat belt and gave her a head mic. "Well, you'll never forget this then!" he said with a big grin. He started up *Menage's Way,* and its engine's deep roar drew much attention. The water lanes were busy, but with a loud foghorn, he made it known that he was coming through. Benita was smiling like a three-year-old as the boat pulled away from the pier. It wasn't about the money, but this guy was doin' the damn thang! Her stomach tightened when Menage made a tight turn and the speedboat sliced through the blue waters. *This is wonderful,* she thought as the wind blew through her hair, feeling the power of his speedboat. The digital speed counter read eighty-five knots. Even though she was strapped in, she gripped the armrest in a death-tight grip as the boat rocketed along the coast. She looked at him smiling, loving the way he took full control of the boat with ease. "This is so cool!" she yelled into her voice mic.

They made it to the restaurant in record time. They ate, talked, laughed, and took turns feeding a tame dolphin that followed them halfway back to Miami. Benita loved everything about Miami, but she thanked God for air conditioning. The smell was always fresh, and just riding a few blocks was an adventure. And the countless malls made Crab Tree look like a flea market. She laughed to herself for even trying to compare Kinston to Miami.

On the way back to the mansion, Menage and Benita's hands joined as the S600 cruised down Biscayne Boulevard. Menage told her that he had to swing by his place to switch to his ESV so he could take Vapor to mate with another Rott in Opalocka. As soon as they pulled up to his mansion, Benita felt butterflies in her stomach. Menage got out first and opened the door for her.

"Thank you," she said stepping out and reaching for his hand. He then led her to the front door. Now, seeing his crib in the daylight, she was speechless. The well-cut lawn . . . even the edges were trimmed. There was no trash in the yard and the neighborhood was quiet. All she could hear was the rustling of the swaying palm trees. They stepped inside and she watched him enter a code into a small keypad, but she didn't see anything happen. The massive living room looked different now, and she eyed Vapor as he lounged on the couch. Benita wasn't too fond of dogs. She moved closer to Menage and squeezed his hand, hoping he'd get the message. He smiled.

"Move, boy." Vapor got up and sat down by his feet. Benita had found out a lot of things about him over their meal, but she could tell he was hiding something. But who didn't?

"So why are you still single?" she asked.

"What do you mean?"

"Boy, please. I know you got mad girls after you, so don't even try to play me!"

"*You* ain't running after me," he shot back. "So tell me more about the course you're taking." He had an hour before he needed to take Vapor to Opalocka, not enough time to please Benita.

"Oh, okay," she said, happy that he was showing an interest in the class she was taking and not her bra size. Solo hadn't asked her once about her course, and as a matter of fact, she didn't even know what she had seen in him. "CMM: It's a class that will give me certification in meeting management. This one lady I know, when I was doing intern work last week, told me she makes seventy-five thousand a year and I can hardly wait to make that kind of money. Anyway, I'd be assisting companies in communicating their brand strategy, but I'll mostly be doing conference meetings and stuff like that. And when I'm not in the books, I love to read and study Greek mythology and—"

"What do you want out of life, Benita?" Menage asked cutting her off.

She was caught off guard. "Well, I. . ." She started to tell him what everybody else would say, happiness, health, love, but he didn't ask her what everyone else wanted; he asked her what *she* wanted. She wanted to one day find true love, settle down, and start a family. But she wondered how much respect he had for her being that she was a stripper. It wasn't like she laid back with her legs open for every nigga that was a so-called baller, or had two or three kids with different fathers. She wasn't about to go down that road full of drama.The only nigga nutting up in her would be her husband. More than half of her coworkers were single parents, and that shit just wasn't cool.

Sure, she wanted Menage, but she had many goals to reach. And what she wanted for her life couldn't be bought. It had to be earned. But yet, deep down, she knew if he had called her the day after he saved her life, she would have had sex with him. She wanted a man to love her and know that she wasn't perfect, nor tried to be. She just wanted someone to commit to and respect her and she would give back her all. But it all boiled down to someone who would love her and never change. Yes, she knew what she wanted out of life, and she also knew the man she wanted *in* her life. But for now she'd keep that to herself.

"You okay, Benita? You kinda zoned out for a minute there."

"Huh? Oh, I'm sorry. It's just that . . . that so much has happened today."

"You sure it ain't about that dude you told me about?" She had told him about Solo and made up a few little white lies about why he was now out of the picture.

He looked at his watch. "Look, I'ma be honest with you. I think you are very down to earth and . . . " He found himself at a loss for words. *And I want to kiss every millimeter of your body,* he wanted to say.

"And what?" she asked in a low whisper.

"I would like to spend more time with you." He wished he could take back his words. What in the hell was he saying? He was supposed to scoop her thick ass up, take her to his bedroom, and dig her back out!

"I don't see a problem with that. But look at the time. I have to get to the train station." He told her to wait a second as he rushed to his bedroom with Vapor on his heels.

"Damn!" he said coming back, Vapor still trailing him.

"What is it?"

"Can't find my damn chain. You ready?"

They rode in his Escalade with Vapor in the back. The ride was too quick for Benita. "I really enjoyed myself today with you, Menage," she said standing by his window. "Bye, Vapor." Vapor poked his head out the window and started barking. Benita jumped back.

"Shut up, boy," Menage ordered. "Look, call me, okay,?" he said touching her shoulder.

"Yeah, I'll do that. Really, I will."

Benita pulled out her keys as she walked to the door of her car. The deep, rumbling bass of the music booming from the Escalade set off the alarm on her car. Benita turned and waved when Menage honked his horn before cruising away. He was now on his way to mate Vapor with another Rottweiler in Opalocka.

***

DJ and Lisa were shopping up in Palm Beach. Well, that's how he played it off to Lisa. He'd met someone who'd do some odd jobs for him if the price was right. Menage had his spot back so moving coke in the stolen cars was dead. But it was all good because DJ had already made enough money to set him on his own two feet, not to mention what he made from the DB-7. He smiled when he saw Lisa walking toward him.

"I'm beat," she said as he took the huge bag from her.

"From what? Spending my paper?" He kissed her on the forehead.

"Oh, you got a problem with that?" she asked putting her hand on her hip.

"Girl, stop trippin'. Let's be out." They headed for the exit.

DJ knew things would work out this time, and Menage would have one last stint in the limelight. As they headed back to Miami, Lisa wondered what the hell Benita had gotten herself into after finding a date-rape pill in her apartment. She hadn't really seemed to be on anything, just acted silly as hell, ranting on and on about sex. *That crazy-ass girl had sex while her period was on, which explained why Solo wasn't around.*

"Drop me off at the house. I have to work tonight," she said reaching for DJ's hand in the dark Jaguar.

"'Bout time you got here," Menage said as Detective Covington followed him into the house. Vapor took off through the living room and ran out back.

"Crazy-ass dog," said Covington. "Yo, man, whatcha got for me?"

"Hold up. I gotta go get that tape. It's in my other car."

Detective Covington sat down in front of the eighty-inch plasma screen. The last time he was here, it looked like a war zone and Menage was in the kitchen hanging on by a thread. His thoughts went back to the tape when Menage returned. After placing it in the slot to be viewed, Menage sat down and picked up the envelope Detective Covington had tossed into his lap. As he tore it open, Detective Covington moved to the edge of his seat.

"Oh, shit! This DJ and Tina! Man, damn, oh, shit!" While Detective Covington watched DJ's Lexus bust through the gate, Menage focused on the pictures in his hand. Tina was playing Dwight, and more than that, he now realized that their relationship wasn't shit. He was convinced now that there was no such thing as love. "I take it that you ain't showed these to Dwight or DJ yet?"

"Nah," Covington said with his eyes glued to the screen. "Can you turn this up?"

Menage turned up the volume by voice command and the tape gained his full attention as DJ got out of his Lex and another guy came into view. Menage's mouth fell open and the pictures slipped from his hands as he watched the two men on screen.

"What the fuck you still doing here? Where the others at?" asked DJ gripping his 9mm at his side.

"The others are all dead, but I hit him," he said quickly.

"Fuck that. Go make sure that muthafucka is dead. Where your heat at, nigga? Ain't 'bout to let a vest save that nigga this time!" DJ moved toward the house, but he stopped and turned around upon hearing Dwight's Viper. Once the gunman turned his back, DJ shot him in the back of his head. The sound brought Vapor to Menage's side in an instant. The tape even showed DJ giving Tina a quick wink before following Dwight into the house. The tape cut off just as the sound of the first police siren was heard. Detective Covington played the tape again as Menage sat still, breathing heavily. His jaws tightened as his temper increased with each passing second. He exploded out of his seat.

"Dem bitch-ass niggas! That nigga put a hit out on me twice! I put all them muthafuckas on and look at what the fuck I get! I'ma see all them bitches. That's my fuckin' word!" he yelled. Grabbing the first thing in sight, he threw a crystal vase against the wall, shattering it.

"Calm down, man."

"Calm down! Calm down! Did you hear what the fuck I just said? I helped all them niggas and that black bitch, Tina! Fuck that! I'ma lay all 'em down." He kicked a chair over. "They wanna play like that . . . man, fuck all this bullshit!"

Detective Covington needed a smoke badly. "Listen. Let's look at it like this: They don't know we have this tape, so they all think everything's still all good. But I can't help you if you go out and catch three bodies tonight. You know that. We need to call Felix. I know he'll come back now, but look man, let's keep this on the down low and play everything cool. And I wouldn't trust any of them over my shoulder if I were you. But trust me, they'll get theirs and you know how my uncle is, so let's go about this the right way. Okay, man? What's it gonna be?"

Menage sucked his teeth. "Yeah, I hear ya, but as soon as you reach Felix, tell him to call me."

"That's a promise. I'll have someone keep a close eye on our friends until we come up with a plan to make them vanish."

Menage turned around and sat his chair upright. "Move, Vapor!"

"I'ma need the tape so I can download it to Felix. You know he'll want to see it. You okay with that?"

"Yeah, 'cause the next time I see any of 'em, I'm bustin'!"

Detective Covington massaged his temples. "Look, just realize that you now have the upper hand in this, so be easy." He searched his pockets for his Newports, forgetting that his wife had thrown them away. "Shit . . . but anyway, we'll have to move fast. And it's a good thing my partner's on leave; I'll have to make this tape vanish. Nah, I'll just put it on another job and erase what's on it, then I'll—"

"Covington, just do your job before I change my fucking mind."

Taking the tape, Covington rushed out the door with his phone to his ear, leaving Menage behind sitting alone in the living room with

Vapor. Menage couldn't believe it. People he
trusted had tried to kill him. His mom always
told him not to trust anyone, but he hadn't taken
heed.

"Go get that thang, boy." Vapor jumped up
and ran to the back. Minutes later he returned,
dragging Menage's MP-10 by its shoulder strap.
"You the only nigga I can trust, boy," he said taking the MP-10. Vapor barked. "Come on, let's
bounce and do it my way, 'cause last time I did it
somebody else's way, I lost Chandra." He stood
up and slung the MP-10 over his shoulder. It
was almost eight when he left with Vapor at his
side. He was wearing a Gucci digital camo
black flight suit with two extra clips for his
MP-10. Putting the top on his Acura Legend,
he let Vapor into the back seat. "They done
fucked up!" he said as he placed the MP-10 on
the passenger's seat. As always, he used music
to express to his mood. Tupac's "Hail Mary"
filled the Acura as it cruised down Seventh
Avenue.

Later that night, he sat in his car under a broken street lamp, looking toward the apartment
down the block. He watched a car pull up and
park at the curb. He was unable to tell what kind
of car it was, but it really didn't matter. He saw
a white girl get out of her car, set the alarm on it
and jog to the apartment. Menage waited a few

minutes before making his move. Picking up his MP-10 and taking off the safety, he screwed on a silencer. Vapor sensed his owner's vibe and whined in the back seat.

"Easy, boy. Just hold it down till I get back," he whispered. Making sure no one was around or peeking through any windows, he got out of the car with the MP-10 hidden under his arm. Looking from left to right, he quickly moved across the street and headed for the apartment.

"Stop playing, DJ! I told you I can't have no hickeys on my neck," the white girl said as DJ reached down between her parted thighs to slide her damp panties to one side. On the table was a line of coke. The two had already snorted four lines and both were feeling the rush. The white girl stripped naked, and DJ pulled out a tube of K-Y jelly and handed it to her as he got up to dim the lights. Moments later he had her face down on the floor as he slid his hard penis into her ass. Since Lisa wasn't into having anal sex, he had to look elsewhere. And this girl had a man, so there were no strings attached. It was kind of funny to him. Tina said she cheated on Dwight because he wouldn't have anal sex with her, let alone eat her ass as she made him do for close to an hour one night. Thinking of Tina made DJ drill the white girl even harder, causing her to cry out. "Shut up, ho, and take it," he said fucking and spanking her ass.

Placing the MP-10 to his chin, Menage squeezed the trigger. The first target was hit. The deadly fusillade tore into the thin sheet metal of the candy red Cadillac Escalade EXT. Moving to the right, he touched up the Platinum Corvette C-5 convertible. Then the Jaguar S-Type R got a new paint job. Changing clips, he let loose rapid fire again. On GP, he tagged the Mazda 626 at the curb also. He took off running and laughing as the alarm went off on the Jaguar. None of the cars could be driven now—busted radiators, flat tires, torn leather seats, windshields caved in, and bullet holes everywhere.

"Stop. . . ah . . . hold up, girl," DJ said trying to pull her off his penis.

"Damn, bitch, hold da fuck up. My alarm going off!" he said pushing her away. She laughed and fell back onto the couch as DJ pulled up his pants and ran to the window. She took another hit of the coke on the table, ignoring him. "Oh, shit!" he yelled, and fell to his knees like a bitch.

***

Menage was keyed up as he ran through a stop sign, speeding down the road with no lights. He made a sharp turn, and the tires squealed as they fought to grip the road. Gunning the engine, he hit the lights and slowed back down when he knew it was clear. *Fuck DJ! Bitch-ass nigga can walk now.* Since the girl he had over was white, Menage hoped they'd blame it on a mad boyfriend or something. Even if DJ thought it could possibly be him, he would ultimately rationalize that Menage would do more than shoot up his whips if he knew he tried to kill him. Menage didn't really give a fuck what he thought. "Damn!" he said when he realized he used up all his ammo for his MP-10, but he still had the Glock-19 and a box of ammo under his seat. He pushed the Legend up to a hundred miles per hour on I-95 while smoking a blunt with his Glock-19 in his lap. All beef would end tonight! He wanted to go back and unload on DJ just stand over him and send him. Fuck Covington and Felix. Fuck a plan. His mind was made up. He pulled up behind Lydia's Maserati and turned out his lights. She greeted him at the door. Even without makeup, she was a pure beauty.

"You okay?" she asked seeing that he was tense. His eyes were bloodshot red. Vapor ignored them both and went inside the apartment.

"He's house trained," Menage said seeing the look on her face. "Leave the lights off . . . please," he added, sitting down and noticing how the sheer blouse she wore brought out her sexy curves. Lydia sat down next to him. When he had called and said he was coming over, she changed out of her boxers and T-shirt.

"You okay?" she asked again, moving closer to him. Menage could see her bright smile in the dark when he put his arm around her and placed it on her bare thigh. He rested his chin on her head.

"I'm so damn tired of this life!"

"What's wrong?" she asked, gently squeezing his thigh.

"You don't wanna get to know me. Everyone looks at me and thinks it's all good because of the shit I have—my Benz, truck, crib. I just don't understand it no more. Ain't shit real. Friends ain't real, love ain't real. Can't trust no fuckin' body. Niggas stabbing me in the back . . . all for the money. There's always somebody trying to get somethin' from me or get close to me. Hell, I don't even know what the fuck my life is for sometimes. After losing my closest friend, I wanted to be alone. Sometimes I wish those bullets hadn't missed my heart, and I mean that. I'm tired of bending over backward for a mutha-fucka—only to get fucked. Taking my kindness for weakness. Niggas wanna change the game? Well, I'ma renovate the shit."

Lydia reached through the dark for his face. "Why? Why are you telling me this?"

"'Cause I know you understand."

Her mind was definitely made up now. She was going to protect him at all costs. But would he trust her? "What happened?" she asked rubbing his chest, wishing that he would hold her tighter.

"Just found out a nigga that's close to me put these marks on my chest."

"Is he in jail?" If not, she sure as hell would make sure that he soon would be.

"Fuck the police, baby girl. I handle my own B.S.—rules of the hood. Well, it's my rule."

Lydia moved her head and strained her eyes to get a good look at him, seeing his face only when a car went by. She felt his pain, his struggle, and she wished they could just leave it all behind. "Are you sure that's a smart thing to do? I mean, I don't wanna see you in no kind of trouble, that's for sure," she said tracing his lips with her finger.

"Girl, you just met me. How you gonna give a fuck about me?"

"Don't judge me if you don't know me, Menage!" she snapped.

"I'm sorry," he said rubbing her ass through the bottom of the thin sheer blouse.

"Better be." She shivered from his touch. "Listen, I didn't ask you to make any promises that you couldn't keep. I don't make plans. I just do life and don't let it get to me. Can you deal with that?"

"Yeah, I can dig it." He kissed her on the forehead as she nuzzled under his chin.

"And no matter what, always remember that I got your back and I'm on your side. You can take that to the bank." Actually, she wanted him to take *her* right now . . . and love her. She moaned something under her breath.

"What?"

"Shhh," she said as she unzipped his shirt. He laid his head back, closing his eyes when he felt her lift up his shirt and place her hot, wet mouth on his chest. Lydia wasn't caught off guard when she came across his Glock-19. Placing it on the table, she started undressing him. No words were spoken as she brought him to life with her hands in the dark living room as a tune by Floetry played in the background.

She parted her legs when he moved between them, kissing her deeply. He gripped the edge of the couch as she reached down to rub his bare penis up and down the folds of her wet sex. When he felt her heels on his back, he slowly began to enter her. He pushed deeper, and she cried out in pain as she locked her arms around his neck. "Take . . . take me, Menage, please." He continued to work slowly, moving into her with long, hard strokes. They rolled to the floor, still joined together, and Lydia ended up on top. Placing her hands on his scarred chest, she let out a deep moan. The deeper he went, the more she wanted him. If the first time he came inside her was a mistake, they made sure the next four times were what they both wanted after they managed to make it to her bedroom. Sweat trickled down her bouncing butt cheeks as he drove into her over and over from behind. Each time he exploded inside her, she fell to her stomach, gripping the pillow as he continued to grind steadily. They later fell asleep, Menage spooning her from behind. She felt wanted and realized that she had crossed a line. She could never go back.

Chapter 5

Still Don't Know

Monday

"Menage, stop, that tickles!" Lydia said rubbing the warm water from her eyes as Menage stood behind her in the shower, twiddling his fingers. He tickled her again, causing her to giggle. She smiled when he wrapped his arms around her, the soapy rag now pressed to her breasts.

"Your friend rising to the occasion again?" she asked feeling his penis bump up against her ass.

"Hey, I ain't got nothin' to do with that. Ain't my fault you got that brown honey bun so close," he whispered in her ear. He watched the water run down her ass cheeks and down her legs. *God, she's sexy*, he thought. "I swear, Latosha, you don't look thirty-two," he said moving the rag down to her stomach. He smiled when he heard her take a deep breath. Since the shower was hitting his back, he carefully switched places with her, allowing the water to rinse from her body. Turning around, she took the still soapy rag from him and started at his brown shoulders. He opened a bottle of scented body wash, poured a little in his hand and grinned at her as he reached down to massage her ass with it. Lydia stepped in closer, still washing him, but she gasped when his penis poked her lower stomach.

"Does that thing ever go down?" she asked moving the rag over his stomach.

"Nah, not until he clears his mind."

"Boy, please. You just horny, that's all," she said looking down at his dick.

"Will you help me out then?" he asked smiling and flicking his nipples.

"Um, don't do that," she said, dropping her free hand down between his legs. Lydia was thankful for the rubber mat in the tub as Menage made love to her in the steamy shower, holding her up against the wall. He was in a daze, watching himself disappear within her pink folds as her small but cute tits pressed against his chest. Again he came inside of her as she yelled out his name, deeply enjoying her own climax.

Menage was fully dressed now, and he walked into the kitchen to find Lydia making him eggs, toast, and grits. "This isn't your mama's cooking, but it will do you some good," she said placing the breakfast in front of him. "Milk or OJ?" she asked giving him a peck on the cheek.

"Some of *your* juice would be fine," he said smacking her on the hip.

"Boy, stop being so darn nasty all the time," she said, knowing she'd strip right now if he told her to. But neither of them wanted to bring up last night's or this morning's unprotected sex.

"Milk will be fine." He was glad she wasn't one of those chicks who was scared to eat in front of a man, because he certainly had no problem asking for seconds.

"Why do you keep looking at my hair?" she asked putting the dishes away after they had eaten.

"Don't see many women these days with real hair," he said getting up and moving behind her, smelling her hair, "so don't cut it and turn around and throw in a weave." Lydia laughed. Was he trying to say that he planned to be around? "What do you want from me, Latosha?" he said turning her around, backing her into the sink.

"For you to just be yourself and realize that you don't have to change anything to please me, and to stay your tail out of trouble. What do you want from me?"

He moved his hand up to her face, tracing her lips with his index finger. He watched her eyes close as her moist lips parted. He didn't want to hurt her, but he knew that last night they had crossed the line. However, he couldn't help but wonder that if she had given it up so fast to him, how many other men had come through and done the same. He was smart and humble enough not to think that it was all about him. But there was something about her other than her stunning body. He just couldn't pinpoint what it was. She took his finger and put it into her mouth. "I don't want much, girl. Just keep your eyes dry and your heart easy. That's all I ask of you."

Menage kissed Lydia long and hard just before stepping out the door with Vapor. "Boy, I'ma put my foot up your butt!" she said laughing into the phone when he called mintues later, telling her that he had borrowed her Floetry CD. She hung up with her heart and mind full of doubt. *Damn!*

"Girl, what the hell am I gonna do with some damn date-rape pill? That shit ain't mine! You got it all wrong!" Benita yelled at Lisa as they stood fussing in the middle of Lisa's bedroom.

"Well, how did it get in here!" Lisa yelled, sticking the pill in her face.

"I said I don't know!"

"Well , who the hell you had up in here, then?"

"Lisa, it's none of your damn business who I have in here!"

"Damn if it ain't! This is my house and you ain't paying shit! I don't need no shit like this in my house! And you know your mom will throw a damn fit if she find out your ass strippin'."

"Well, damn, I guess Keith will tell her now as loud as you're yelling!"

Lisa looked to the living room where their cousin was. "He ain't gonna say shit. But back to you! You need to get your act together. Is this what you took at the party?"

"What?"

"Girl, you was really trippin' and you didn't smell like no wine or nothing. You just . . . it was odd, girl," Lisa said lowering her voice. "I'm trying to look out for you, that's all. I'm sorry."

Benita slowly sat down on the bed. She knew whose pill it was. Solo was the only man ever to set foot in Lisa's bedroom. *Could he have slipped something in my drink?*

"Hey, Benita, I got your chain," yelled Keith as he followed Lisa outside. He'd found the platinum medallion on the dresser, and he would front like it was his at the mall Lisa was taking him to.

"Yeah, yeah," Benita said paying him no mind. "And stay outta my damn stuff!" she yelled. He ignored her last remark. She got up and called Solo but he didn't answer. She paged him and waited. "If it ain't one thing it's another," she told herself. Flopping back down onto the bed and tossing a pillow over her face, she let out a loud scream. But she knew she had to control her anger and not let it control her. She had class. However, she'd be working her shift at the strip club soon. Bills had to be paid.

"When did this happen, man?" Dwight said into the phone, sitting behind his desk at MD Beauty Salon.

"Last night 'round ten. I didn't hear the shots, but like I said, once the alarm went off, I went and looked out the window," DJ replied.

"Damn!" So all your whips are totaled. And you don't have no idea who it was?"

"I had this chick over. She said her boyfriend is like that. Shit, her whip was shot up too!"

"Lisa know about it? Y'all guys gon' learn to stop creeping on your girls," Dwight said, conveniently forgetting about that night with Latosha.

"Yeah, I know that's right!" DJ said thinking of Tina. "You told Menage yet?"

"I called him right after it went down, but he didn't answer his cell or page," DJ lied.

"Shit, you know he don't answer if he's with a woman, and that's most of the time. But what are you gonna do? Wanna use my BMW till you get on your feet? I can't let you push the Viper," he laughed.

"Nah, I'm straight. Been stackin' dough, you know. Matter of fact, I'm in Fort Lauderdale looking at something to cop now. Yo, how much that Bentley run?"

"About two hundred thou' with all the rims and custom seats."

"Well, I'm about to cop this black Volvo V-70R wagon, throw some twenty-two's on it, toss in a system, and call it a day for now."

"Well, when you get straight, call me back and let me know what's up, okay? And thanks for calling."

"Yeah, peace out, yo!"

Dwight hung up shaking his head and went back to work.

Tina was in her office talking to Akissi.

"Yes, I know it's spur of the moment. But I want to surprise Dwight, so tell everyone to keep their mouths shut, mainly that big mouth Jamal."

"That ain't the only thing that's big on him," Akissi said blushing.

"Uh-uh, no you didn't, girl! When this happen?"

At Menage's pool party. We went to his place afterwards. And girl, he can work that tongue," Akissi added snapping her fingers. They laughed and gave each other a high five across the desk.

"Well, I'm counting on you to have things set up, okay?"

"You said you'll call Menage?" Akissi asked.

"Yeah," Tina lied, knowing good and well she wasn't going to call him. She'd die first before inviting Menage to the party. "I'll call him myself. You know how close he and my baby are."

"Well . . . uh, put a word in for me."

"With who, girl?"

"Sexy-ass Menage. I'm tired of hearing Tylisha brag about him!"

"Girl, please! Get your hot ass out of here . . . but I'll see what I can do." Tina smiled slyly.

"How far are you, anyway?" Akissi asked standing up to leave.

"Two weeks. Hey, when I have to stay at home I'm putting you in charge, all right?"

"Thanks, Tina."

"Nah, girl, you earned it, as hard as you work. You got that guest list, right?" Akissi slapped the pocket on her hip and turned to leave the office. Once the door was closed, Tina leaned back in her seat and rubbed her stomach. She hoped it was a girl. *Life couldn't get any better,* she thought.

Chapter 6

Same Ol' Bullshit

Menage watched the car carrier unload his new ride that was still covered. After it was placed in his garage, he signed for it and went back inside to get out of the beaming heat. Detective Covington had called him a few minutes earlier and went off on him because he knew he had shot up DJ's cars. He told him that Felix would be in Thursday night if nothing changed. He also told him about DJ's new Volvo and that someone from the family had a tag on him. Menage promised he'd stay cool until Felix arrived. But judging by the way he'd torn his bedroom apart looking for his medallion, he was anything but cool.

Even though he had just left Latosha, he was ready to see her again. Just thinking of her made him hard. Sitting at his high powered computer, he checked all of his accounts. After dropping close to half a mill on his new car, he was left with over a million dollars, not counting the fifteen grand from the card game over at Coonk's place Friday night. He really didn't have to work, so what else was there to do other than get sex every day? And that was far from played out. Same line, different chick, over and over.

He thought about the pictures of DJ and Tina and for a second he thought about how much fun DJ probably had with her. He'd never do Dwight like that. Even if Tina had made a move on him, like she did once before, he still wouldn't do it. But DJ obviously didn't give a damn. *Fuck them.* "CD four, song three." Seconds later, Nappy Roots filled the mini mansion.

Just as a drug dealer was never supposed to use his own products, Menage had a rule to never ride in a tagged car. All of his were bought and paid for. Even if he closed the shop, he'd still have money coming from MD Beauty Salon to take care of all his needs. Did Dwight have a part in trying to kill him? He sure as hell would have a motive. He'd have full control of everything. But what part did that bitch, Tina play? Something had to change. He needed Chandra, but he forced her from his mind. "I swear, there's gotta be more to life than this," he said reaching down to rub Vapor behind his ears. Going through his e-mail, he smiled when he saw that he had a message from Passion. After sending her back a short message, he fed Vapor and pulled out a green sweatsuit by Iceberg with a Fedora to match. He felt naked without his name piece. He stepped outside into the humid air and called Dough-Low, who answered on the third ring.

"Yo, what's up? Where you at?" Menage asked.

"Opalock, on the block, doin' my thang."

"What, Ali-Baba?" He glanced at his Bulova. It was almost two thirty.

"Yeah, you comin' through?"

"Might as well. Ain't shit else to do."

"Do that, cuz. By the way, stop at the sto' and get me some Dutch Masters."

"Got that."

"Hurry up. Later on we can dip over to my girl crib. Her cousin is down from VA, fine as fuck."

"Bet!" Menage said clipping his Nokia on his waist as he got into his S600. Close to an hour later, he pulled up behind Dough-Low's Hummer H2 with his system banging. Stepping out of his ride, he joined Dough-Low on the corner where he sat on a milk crate that sunk in from the weight of his body.

"'Bout time you got here," Dough-Low said reaching for the Dutch Masters. Menage flipped a crate on its side and sat down. Behind them sat a group of females on a crowded porch, smoking weed and tripping out. A few shorties were playing down the street in a mango tree, tossing down the rotten fruit or trying to catch some lizards, which was how he used to pass the time back in the day in Liberty City.

Menage didn't feel that Dough-Low was helping the hood by pushing dope, but didn't those who worked for him have food on their tables and clothes on their backs? They had to risk the everyday hustle as well as the DT's or another nigga filled with hate. Dough-Low had his game and Menage had his. But both had seen the worst of life and realized that Mary J. Blige said it right on the money: Life can be only what you make it.

"So what's really goin' on?" Menage asked reaching for the blunt.

"Yo, dis cat said some fools pulled off on him wif two Os last week, and I got word they 'pose ta hit the block today. But I got a little surprise fo' 'em!" Dough-Low said rubbing the butt of his .45.

Menage passed the blunt back and told Dough-Low about DJ.

"D-dat . . . bitch . . . ass nigga!" Dough-Low coughed and beat his chest, trying to talk as smoke billowed from his mouth.

"If you didn't roll this shit so damn tight you wouldn't be choking!" Menage laughed and took the blunt from Dough-Low.

Menage started to feel the blunt's effect. When he said he needed to piss, Dough-Low pointed over his shoulder. "Katasha will let you use the bathroom. She's the big girl wif the blue weave."

Menage walked up on the porch and asked Katasha if he could use the bathroom. She said yes and made some explicit remarks behind his back as he went inside. Finding the small bathroom, he quickly relieved himself as he closed his eyes and tilted his head back. He was shaking himself just as the black shower curtain slid back. Menage stood over the toilet with his penis in his hand as a thick redbone stood in the shower, dripping wet. There was no sign of shock on her face.

"I had just turned the water off when you came in," she said, ignoring the fact that she was naked in front of a stranger. She slowly stepped out of the shower with a look of hunger in her eyes. "Nice," she said looking at his dick. Menage stood inches from her as she dried herself off. "You the guy with the Benz, right?" she asked as her nipples became hard. He nodded yes and started to feel the rise between his legs. She watched him grow. "I never seen you 'round here before . . . I guess this is an odd way to meet, huh?" she asked, unconsciously licking her thick lips. She turned around, grabbed a towel and rubbed it over her wet, plump ass. "Dry my back for me?" She figured this was the quickest way to the passenger's seat of his S600. He reached for the towel and did as she had asked.

"Fuck this," he said, tossing the towel to lick her neck while sliding his dick up and down between her butt cheeks.

"Ooh, it's so hard and hot," she said, arching her ass toward him. "Some rubbers in the cabinet," she panted, reaching through her parted legs to wrap her fist around him. "I don't even . . . know your name," she said jerking him off as he cupped her wet breasts and licked the back of her neck.

"Menage," he said moving his hips back and forth as she tightened her grip.

"Mine's Tatiana. Mmm, I want this dick." She released her grip and turned around to jack him off some more.

Damn, this must be my lucky day, Menage thought.

After strapping up, he got back behind her with his pants around his ankles. Tatiana bit her bottom lip and looked over her shoulder at Menage. "Beat my nookie good." When he slid into her, she grabbed hold of the towel rack and began to moan. He held onto her smooth waist and started long-stroking her with every inch he had to give. Feeling her legs go out from under her, he moved closer to the wall, still taking her from behind and gripping her waist even tighter. Even through the condom he could feel how tight and wet she was inside. Pushing him back as he continued to stroke her, she managed to get down on her hands and knees.

"That was good," Tatiana said stepping back into the shower as Menage cleaned himself off with a warm rag. "You got me so weak." She parted her legs, letting the water hit her sex. Before he left, she called him to the edge of the tub to wrap her small, lotion-coated fist around his penis to serve up round two, which ended up on her chin and the top of her breasts. "Be sure to keep me in your thoughts," she said smiling before putting her head under the streaming water.

When Menage walked back outside, the group of girls on the porch all got quiet.

"Damn, what you do in there?" one of them asked, breaking the silence.

His head was still tight from the weed. "Say what?" he asked smelling his fingers.

"Smells like pussy to me. He been fuckin' I bet! I told you, girl, I heard some moanin' in there," said another one of the girls. Menage was about to kick game, but Dough-Low called him from the corner.

"Damn, you use my bathroom and I don't get no play. What's up wit' dat?" Katasha said rolling her neck. Menage told Dough-Low to hold up for a second as he pulled Katasha inside her crib. He took her straight to the bathroom where Tatiana was. Tatiana had told him about her cousin, Katasha, and her freaky ways, and she hit it right on the money when she had said that Katasha might try to push up on him. Katasha was a little over-weight, and she figured Menage would dis her, but she found out that she was wrong as he bent her big black ass over and hit it from the back. It got so crazy that he even pulled out a piece *of* her weave. He left Tatiana in the tub, playing with herself, and Katasha on the floor curled up in a ball.

"Nigga, you'd fuck yourself to death if you got the chance!" Dough-Low said shaking his head.

"Anybody come through yet?" Menage asked smelling his fingers.

"Nah, not yet. But I know they will. Greed with sticky fingers will make a nigga slip." He lit a new blunt and passed it to Menage.

"Let's bounce over to the strip club tonight," Menage said taking a pull on the blunt.

Dough-Low didn't hear him. He was looking down the street.

"Yo, yo, yo, that's them bitch fools right there," he said pulling out his .45 as a green Navigator slowed to a stop about a block and a half away. "You got your heat?"

"Yeah," Menage said flicking the blunt to the ground. "We'll sit in the whips and see how it goes down!"

Both men sat in their cars and eyed the Navigator. Dough-Low watched one of his workers step up to the driver's side window. After exchanging a few words with the driver, he ran back across the street to grab a bag from another guy sitting on a packed porch. Looking back over his shoulder, then up and down the street, he sprinted back across the street to make the sale. It happened fast. As soon as the bag was placed through the front window, the barrel of a pump stuck out the back window and exploded with a loud boom as the kid fell dead in the street. The next blast was aimed at the Navigator as the SUV sped forward. Dough-Low didn't waste a second to step out and unload his .45 through the Navigator's windshield. The SUV would have made it past the .45, but Menage's MP-10 started to chatter as he let loose a full burst, standing through the sunroof of his S600. He stayed on the trigger, stitching the Navigator, busting its headlights and punching holes in the hood. The tires locked as it swerved then slammed into a pole. Menage started to change his clip and get out, but Dough-Low was already running toward the wrecked Navigator, his .45 leading the way. The driver fell out with blood flowing down his face.

"H-help me, man, I got kids. I didn't—"

The roar of Dough-Low's .45 finished him. Dough-Low didn't show any remorse, nor did he look to see whether the other two were alive or not as he dumped the entire clip on the passenger and the guy in the back. Running back to his SUV, he motioned to Menage that it was time to be out. This was Dough-Low's hood, so he had to issue a full payback plus he knew the kid who now lay down the street with half his chest missing from a point blank range shot from a pump. Both cars made quick U-turns, making their exit.

Menage later found himself in Kamesa's bathroom, splashing cold water on his face. He wished he was like Dough-Low conscience free but he wasn't. Four niggas dead over some bullshit. The KKK would be happy, niggas killing their damn selves. It made him sick. He tried to think of something else.

"What the fuck are you doing?" he asked looking into the mirror. "Sitting on a mill and still out on the block bullshitting." Getting himself together and walking toward the living room, he passed the half-closed door of Kemesa's bedroom. He could see her head hitting the headboard of her bed and heard loud banging of the wood against the wall as Kemesa's moans matched Dough-Low's grunting. Kemesa's cousin, Sherika, was sitting in the living room filing her pink nails. She was average looking and appeared to be in her late thirties. She was about five feet three inches and had a nice little ass, but her hips were thick. Her hair was done in braids that were piled on top of her head. With a quick glance, Menage gave her a seven on a scale from one to ten, but he bumped her score up to an eight upon seeing how clear her beautiful dark skin was. She was relaxed in a pair of stone washed Baby Phat jeans and scoop neck tee.

"You feeling okay?" she asked patting a spot next to her on the couch.

"Yeah, just got a lot on my mind. Sherika, right?"

"Yes, Kemesa told me a few things about you, nothing personal, though," she said glancing at him. They both looked down the hall, hearing the bed now crashing harder into the wall. "I guess Dough-Low has a lot on his mind too," Sherika said touching his knee. Menage could only shrug his shoulders.

"I see you got a six outside. I'm supposed to buy one next year. I have the ESS AM6 model now," she said crossing her legs.

"Doin' it, ain't cha?" he asked.

Sherika went on to tell him that she was a radiologist, divorced mother of one, and in her first year of college. She also told him that she loved young men, mainly those who would 'dine at the Y,' a term she used for oral sex. "So, you and Dough-Low go way back?"

"Yeah, we do," he said slumping back on the couch. Thinking about the fact that he had just been involved with three murders, his mind really wasn't on the girl sitting next to him.

"Mmm," she moaned just as her pink Baby Phat cell phone on the coffee table chimed. After saying hello, she lowered her voice. He knew it was some dude, and it gave him his chance to bounce.

"Tell Dough-Low to page me," he said heading for the door. He saw that she wanted to say something, but she could only nod her head. He jumped into his S600, and checked the time. It was just after four thirty. He drove home in silence.

Pulling up in his driveway, he nearly jumped out of his skin when a horn sounded behind him. Looking into his rearview mirror, clutching his Glock-19, he looked at the Chrysler Crossfire parked in front of his gate and saw an arm waving at him. It took a second for him to realize that it was Benita.

"What's up with you, Mr. Legend?" she asked dropping her Miss Sixty backpack on the plush rug inside his living room. She wore a red Baby Phat terrycloth jumpsuit. Menage had walked into the house behind her, shaking his head at the shape of her body. He would drink her bath water.

"Chillin', 'nother day, 'nother dollar," he said sitting next to her on the couch taking out his cornrows.

"Sorry I didn't call yesterday, but I got so busy with my cousin. I didn't come at a bad time, did I? I was in the area, so I figured I'd stop by plus I'm just getting out of class."

"Nah, it's okay. I need some company anyway," he said, wondering if she came over just to fuck. "Hey, what kind of book is that?" he asked pointing to her open bag on the rug.

"Greek Mythology. Remember I told you it's what I study in my spare time?"

"Greek Mythology . . . tell me more about it." He let out a deep breath and dropped his tired arms.

Benita smiled and leaned forward to get the book. "Trust me, you'll like it," she said passing him the book. "Like Zeus. We deal with the concept every day and don't even know it. It's very interesting," she added looking at him flip through her book. *Any other guy would be trying to flip me on my back by now,* she thought, enjoying every second with him. She gazed past his head and looked toward the backyard. "I don't believe it!" she said standing up.

"What?" Menage asked looking at her and following her gaze. All he saw was Vapor out back lying on his stomach, chewing on an old pair of shoes.

"Come on," she said reaching for his hand, "and bring the book also." Following her outside, he looked down at the size of her butt. *It just don't make no damn sense,* he thought. Vapor looked at them for a second then went back to his shoe. They stopped at a row of yellow flowers near the patio.

"Do you know what these are?" she asked not realizing that she was squeezing his hand.

"Uh, some yellow flowers I guess," he said shrugging his shoulders.

Her smile made his stomach flutter. "No, it's not just some yellow flowers. It's called a Chinese Sacred Lily, a variety of the Polyanthus Narcissus. A daffodil is also a polyanthus. Anyway, Narcissus was a Greek youth. It's a myth now, but the story goes like this: Narcissus was so into himself and his own image. He looked at his reflection in a pond one day and he was changed into this flower. That's why it bears his name. So the word narcissism is like . . . let's say someone who think they all that."

I must be all that, you got your phat ass over here, he thought.

"Turn to page one-eighty-seven," said Benita smiling.

"Damn," Menage said when he got to the page, "you know your stuff, huh?"

"You can say that," Benita said smiling again. She smiled a lot when she was with Menage. "Who picked this flower out for you?"

"This lady I hired to do all the other stuff. Now I see she was tryin' to be funny," Menage said, letting her hand go to touch the flower. He pulled another one and gave it to her. "For you . . . for being the opposite of this flower," he said being as smooth as he could be. She took it and looked into his eyes. Here she stood with this man, alone in his backyard as the sun beamed down on the two of them. She wanted him, she couldn't lie, but she wouldn't throw herself on him.

"Thank you." She smelled the flower and looked up at him before quickly breaking their eye contact. He was about to say to hell with it and kiss her, but she suddenly gasped.

"That statue on top of the birdbath, don't tell me you don't know who that is!"

He looked at the statue and smiled. "I don't know, but she has some nice tits."

"Funny," she said pinching his arm. "You have so much Greek mythology right here in your backyard and you don't even realize it."

"School me, then," Menage said taking her hand without thinking.

Benita walked toward the statue. "It's Aphrodite, the goddess of love and beauty, also called Cytherea."

"Hmm . . . well I should call you Cytherea," he said stuffing the book into his pocket.

"Only if you let me call you Adonis." She turned to face him, tilting her head to one side.

"Why?"

"Because he's the one Cytherea fell in love with," she said leaving out the fact that Aphrodite fell for Adonis based on his good looks. "So you see, Greek mythology is everywhere, but you just don't see it. I'm sure you have a pair of Nikes. Nike is the Greek goddess of victory. You can look through the book if you'd like."

Menage grabbed her other hand and changed the subject. "Why did you come here, Benita?"

Her mouth closed then opened again, but she didn't say anything. However, she refused to break away from his gaze this time. "Because I wanted to be around you." His thumb rubbing the back of her hand made goose bumps form all over her body. *Why wasn't he like the rest, all out for sex? Then she could put him in his place,* she thought. She didn't know how to handle this. She began feeling aroused.

"Let's go back inside, Benita," Menage said. His sexy voice had her wishing that he could just talk to her forever. She squeezed his hand and pulled him close, her breasts pressing into his chest as Vapor ran past them toward the house. They both smiled at Vapor.

Back inside the house, Menage sat between her soft thighs as she took out the rest of his cornrows and greased his scalp. Vapor was running up and down the halls, shaking the old shoe in his mouth.

"What's on your mind?" she asked dipping two fingers into the jar of grease next to her.

"Just thinkin' 'bout life, that's all," he said with his eyes closed.

She tapped his head so he could lean to the left and rest on the towel draped over her thigh. "And?" she asked parting his hair with the comb, then going back for more grease.

Menage sighed. "Well, Benita, it's hard, to tell the truth. I don't know. I guess I just have to take things one day at a time just take what's given, you know?"

"Sort of. But have you ever thought about maybe taking things in life that you want instead of just taking what's given?" She went on before he could answer. "All your life, Menage, and stop me if I'm wrong, you've been the one to take care of people and you've always been the person everyone's called and depended on. But the truth is, you don't have anyone to hold your own back, to hold you down or catch you if you fall. Am I right?"

Menage replied quickly. "Don't need nobody but my dog!" He rubbed Vapor's side as he lay next to him. Benita ignored his answer.

"Are you happy with your life? Is your soul content? Boy, you saved my life, and I'm not only gonna *do* your head, I'ma get *in* it!" she said popping his shoulder with the comb.

"Is that right?" he asked with a smirk.

"Can't get no righter," she laughed. "What do you see yourself as?" She tapped his head to the right while popping her fingers.

"A fool, I guess," he said closing his eyes as she continued to do his hair.

"No, a legend," she said softly. "A legend is what you want to be. A unique one at that. Living up to your name, you can say, huh?"

"I just live from day to day, Benita," he said unable to ignore her soft thighs.

"Listen, Menage, you can't bring me down with your problems, so open up to me, okay? We can lift each other up, you feel me? If there's something you want to talk to me about, I'm all ears. Believe me, I'll be that friend you never had. I'll listen and respond when you need me to. There's a lot you can learn from me just as I can learn from you. I'm still even learning to fully express myself. But I'll be here for you."

Menage listened to every single word she said, but with each word, she added another brick to the wall around his heart. "And to answer your question from the other day . . . well, what I want out of life is true love. I pray for the love my heart desires, and there's only one man on this earth that can give it to me. I don't want no other man, other than the one that's for me. I desire to be loved, Menage, so bad that if the true love I found was a light, no one could stand the brightness of it. You feel me? Love is a very strong subject for me. There's some ways I feel about love that just can't be put into words. I'm willing to do whatever I have to do to experience true love."

Menage sat between her legs with his eyes shut tightly. He couldn't understand why she was talking about something that wasn't real. In his book, love wasn't nothing but a bullshit four letter word. And he planned to prove it to her.

As soon as she was done with his hair, he turned to face her, still on his knees. He looked deeply into her eyes. Their faces were now only a few inches apart. "Love ain't real, Benita," he said.

"I can change your mind." She touched his arm.

"Never happen!"

"Just let me know what you want to do. You can turn to me when you want to talk or just vent. I'll be your strength when you're weak.

"I don't need it. Life won't give it to me."

"Why wait for life to give it to you?" If you have a need then fulfill it. Maybe what you think you have to wait to be given to you is waiting for you to just take it. And sometimes if you wait too long, you'll miss out—especially in love. And as far as that goes, I love with my soul and spirt . . . and my heart. Most men no, most boys don't understand that." Benita had Menage against the wall.

"Well, how would I . . . I mean, a man, know it's real?"

"The man that I choose will know my love is real, and he'll understand it to the fullest. I'll not only want to know his mind, but I'll explore his soul and spirit. I know you, Menage. You don't think your words say a lot but they do. I listen to everything you say. Yes, other guys step to me, but I don't get the same feeling from them that I get from you. And I' m not going to question it." Benita slowly reached up and touched the side of his face. "I can't ignore what I feel for you, Menage. She looked away for a moment and then back at him. "You don't have to look for true love because it will expose itself. See, you made me say more than I wanted to." Benita's heart was racing and she took a long, deep breath. Menage closed his eyes and lowered his head as Benita's small, soft hands rubbed the back of his neck. Her touch melted him, causing him to let out a deep breath.

"Thanking you every day for the rest of my life, that's what I want to do, Menage. Do you feel uncomfortable?" she asked running her nails up and down the nape of his neck. He shook his head no, but he had to fight her and this thing called love. He raised his head and looked back into her eyes. He moved in closer to her. Benita closed her eyes and opened her mouth. Their lips and tongues met and they kissed each other hungrily.

"I want you now, Benita," Menage said without breaking their kiss. With his palms placed under her elbows, he brought her to her feet. Still kissing her, he scooped her up and carried her to the place where he planned to break her—his bed.

In a rundown hotel in Overtown, Scorpion finally awoke. His head was still throbbing, but the rage inside him drove him on. Since the night he jumped from the small Augusta 109 helicopter seconds before it exploded, he had slowly regained his strength. It was by sheer luck that the moon's reflection on the aircraft caused him to notice that something wasn't right. He had veered hard to the left, taking the helicopter lower, but the flickering light moving in his direction left no doubt in his mind that he had to bail and do it fast. The two mercenaries never knew what hit them. He had somehow made it to land from ten miles out or so on a floating plank of wood. His brain disorder condition was now at a point of no return. Scorpion sought revenge.

He laid on his back and turned to look at the lanky blonde prostitute next to him. The room stank from the stopped up toilet and the smell of dead fish. The woman didn't mind; she stopped caring hours ago when Scorpion had tightened the steel garrote collar around her neck. The air conditioner was at least working, filling the dark, small room with cool air and delaying rigor mortis. Scorpion rolled over on top of the woman, placing his penis back inside of her cold body . . . and started pumping.

"Hey, Covington," said FBI agent, Todd Davis, as he entered his office.

"Yeah, what's up?" Covington asked nodding toward the chair in front of his desk.

Agent Davis laid a folder on his desk. "A friend of mine in L.A. called me a few weeks back and asked me if we had anything on that guy . . . uh . . . Menage, but we didn't. But I'll let you look at it. Apparently, the Mayor's son was killed and his car was stolen."

"Did they do a follow-up?" Covington asked, staying calm and cool at the mention of Menage's name by the feds.

"Don't know. But since I owe you a favor I thought I'd let you know about it. Maybe he was shot over that or it might not be a connection at all. Well, that's what they faxed to me and you can keep that copy. I have another," Davis said.

Covington kept his questions limited, and when Davis left he felt the urge to light up a Newport, but he didn't. He also knew he couldn't use his land or cell phone to call Menage and give him a heads up about the FBI. He didn't know that Davis had left out the info about the undercover agent already on the case. Putting the fax to the side, he got back to work, hoping Menage would keep his nose clean until he could reach him later.

Menage watched Benita step out of his bathroom wrapped in a terry cloth towel. He swallowed as his eyes traveled over her body.

"I'm . . . r-ready," she said nervously. Stepping into his embrace, she closed her eyes as he slid his hands under the towel. Menage gently kissed the drops of water on her collar bone as he ran his fingers along the edge of her thong. "Close your eyes," she whispered into his ear. Stepping back, he closed his eyes, knowing his throbbing erection was showing through his boxers. He thought they were about to go at it when they had first entered the bedroom earlier, but Benita pulled away to go to the shower. "Okay, you can look now." Benita spoke in such a sweet voice that Menage thought he felt his heart skip a beat. He opened his eyes and found her standing before him, clad in a white garter belt and a white fishnet bra that separated her full breasts. She was luscious in all of the right places, and right now he only wanted to be inside of her. He eased toward her, and his hands moved to the front clasp of her bra to remove it as her hand slid between his legs. Hearing her heavy panting, he slid his tongue over her left nipple and wished that time could stand still. She looked impeccable, with thick thighs and a wide and soft butt that seemed to spill through his fingers. Piece by piece, she allowed him to remove her clothing. Stepping out of her thong, she felt his penis bump between her legs as he feasted on her neck while cupping and squeezing her breasts. Menage led her to his bed and he sat down. He turned her around and told her to bend over at the waist and rest her elbows on his dresser.

"Just trust me, baby," he said rubbing her soft butt cheeks that were smooth as silk from her bi-weekly Brazilian wax. Running her fingers through her hair, she did as he asked. "Menage," she purred when she felt his hands move over her back and down her thighs. She felt so exposed as he sat behind her, commenting on and admiring her body. When he slid a finger between her lips, she became tense. "Relax," he said as he slowly moved his finger back and forth. "Menage," she purred over and over. He fingered her until her legs became weak, and he replaced his fingers with his tongue as his hands cupped her dangling breasts. Benita couldn't believe what he was doing to her. She had heard Lisa and the other girls at the club talking about getting their pussies eaten, but there were no words to describe the pleasure she was feeling right now. Reaching back with one hand to place it on the back of his head, she started to grind into his face. "O-h-h . . . y-e-s-s-s," she panted. "Mmmm." Menage had Benita intoxicated as he pulled her butt cheeks apart to tongue her asshole, and she popped the first condom in her eagerness to get it on him. After replacing it with a new one, he remained seated on the bed and beckoned her to come and sit on his lap. Straddling his legs and facing him now, she slowly lowered herself onto him. "I . . . I can't," she said with him halfway inside of her. Menage was surprised at how tight she was. There was no way she could be a virgin.

"I want you so fuckin' bad, girl," he said pushing between her thighs.

"Don't hurt me," she said reaching down to guide him inside her. He slid into her and held his breath. She dug her nails into his shoulders, and she called out his name as she received each inch of his hardness. Feeling her soft thighs rubbing against his, he slowly began stroking her. She gripped him like a glove. He started grinding her hard and fast, ignoring her cries that soon turned into her pleading for more. Rolling her hips to match his strokes, her eyes rolled in her head as the intense pleasure started to build up between her thighs. His penis drove over and over into her sex, and her breasts bounced with each of his driving strokes. Pumping her steadily as her nails created marks on his shoulders, he kissed her, sliding his tongue in and out of her mouth. "Oh, Menage!" she screamed, arching her back to take him in deeper. "Do it, do it!" she yelled as he created a new position, laying her across the bed onto her back and throwing her legs over his shoulders. Then he rolled over onto his back and let her ride him. On and on they continued while keeping a steady pace. Menage later took her standing and on the floor, and he again pumped her from behind and ate her pussy.

"You okay, girl?" he asked as he strapped up again.

"Yeah, why you ask?" she asked lying on her side.

"You just . . . never mind," he said reaching out to play with a nipple. Benita looked at him, wondering what he thought of her. She wasn't stupid or naive. She knew that good sex didn't mean love. This was what she wanted, and it was her main reason for coming.

"You like this, don't you?" she asked looking into his eyes as she straddled him once again. "Don't answer. Just let me show you my gratitude for saving my life," she said leaning forward to stick her tongue in his ear. "I want you to do something."

"What is it?"

"You'll be my first."

"First for what?" Ignoring his question, she spun around, preparing to get into the six-ty-nine position. Closing her eyes, she lowered her mouth onto his throbbing penis. "Gotdamn!" he said feeling her lips locking around his penis.

Since Menage didn't believe in love, nor try to find it, the wall he had put up around his heart was still there when Benita brought up the subject of starting something. Benita was in love and Menage was far from it. She didn't want to leave, but her cousin had called and told her he'd locked himself out of the house after going to the corner store for some Black and Milds. He also told her that Lisa had left with some dude in a Volvo. "Dang, boy, I'm on my way," Benita said before ending the call. Menage refused to let her leave so fast. After getting her fully stim-ulated with his tongue, he took her again with his hands around her waist, drilling her hard and fast from behind. He cupped her jiggling tits and grunted as he released himself inside her fist tight sex. He hated to see her phat ass leave, but as soon as she pulled out of his gate, he was in the shower washing off her scent. Within thirty minutes he was stepping outside in a pair of Ecko baggy jeans and pullover with shoes to match. He jumped in his Acura and banged his system.

Menage called Dough-Low and found out that he was still in Carol City. He was on his way to *Bounce Back,* but he changed his mind when Sherika shouted in the background that she wanted to finish where they had left off. Driven to live up to his name, Menage made a detour.

He ran his fingers over Sherika's breasts as she nuzzled his neck. She introduced him to a new sex game: Flip the coin. "If it's heads, we have to give each other oral sex simultaneously. But if it's tails, then we go at it in any position," she said smacking his ass. The first flip was tails, and she mounted and rode him while looking into his eyes, her tits dangling in his face. Her rhythm revealed that she had lots of experience. She was so wet that he could feel her juices running down between his legs. "Aw, baby, tell me it's good to you," she said as sweat rolled off her nipples and Menage nibbled on them. She fell to her elbows, still rocking her hips over him. "Menage," she moaned, speeding up her movement. "Mmm, damn, I'm going to nut, I'm going to nut!" She did and rolled over onto her back afterward, but he stayed with her and took control, placing one of her legs up over his shoulder.

"My world!" he said as she began speaking a new language.

Chapter 7

Maybe If I Was There . . .

The party at Dwight and Tina's condo was in full swing. Lisa was on top of the world, wearing a stunning Dolce and Gabana backless body suit, sipping a glass of Hynotiq. DJ stood behind her with his hands on her hips, wearing Versace jeans, Tims and a Vintage CCCP red hockey jersey. Tina turned every head, wearing a beautiful iridescent yellow, silk organza pleated decollete midriff top with raglan sleeves and a pair of tight-fitting Jowrider jeans, all by Prada. She smiled at Dwight as he stood in the den, decked out in an Armani suit. He was the happiest man in the world. Tina had just told their guests that she was having his baby, which was the reason for the surprise party. And Dwight surprised her and everyone else by saying that he wanted to jump the broom in July instead of next year as they had planned.

Lydia sat at the bar drinking Moët, thinking about Menage. She was in love with damn boy. And for that reason she welcomed the opportunity to get out and unwind, to be in a different atmosphere. In addition to that, she had the chance to cop the fly Fendi strapless dress she wore. Dwight was no longer a concern of hers, and she didn't appear to even notice him.

Jamal was in the bathroom with Akissi. She straddled his lap on the toilet, her dress bunched up at her waist, as he sat with his pants down around his ankles. His mind was so caught up in being up Akissi's ass that he had forgotten to show Dwight the picture he had of Lydia as a Jet Beauty. There was no doubt in his mind that it was Lydia, who they had come to know as Latosha. But what had really caught his attention was the short bio on her; she had attended the FBI academy. Jamal didn't know she was at the party. Not getting enough friction, he told Akissi to lie on her back. "Come on, shug," he said parting her thighs.

"Nigga, you need to hurry up," she said watching him slide back into her as they lay on the bathroom rug. "Uh! You big-dick fucker!" Her nails dug into his ass as he started pumping her again.

"I know that's right!" he said drilling her like a rabbit.

***

Lydia knew there was a tie between Tina and DJ. And once again she thought about what the girl in the salon had said about Tina sneaking around behind Dwight's back. Was it with DJ? Her baby, yes, that's what she called Menage now, had someone watching his back, protecting him from spending a long ass time in prison and he didn't even know it. How would he react to the truth? God she didn't want to lose him. She thought about telling him that she loved him. *Yeah, right. He'd laugh in my* face, she thought. But didn't their last night of sex mean anything to him? Well, it did to her when she felt him cumming inside her as she rode him. *Damnit, just call him,* she thought to herself. No, she didn't want to waste any time. She wanted to see him face-to-face and then naked. This man was driving her crazy and she loved every second of it. She would see him tonight no matter how late it was. First she'd make love to him. She'd make sure to do it good. And maybe she'd even suck him. She imagined saying, "Fuck it, nigga, I love you," and then coming clean. She crossed her legs at the mere thought of how he would make her feel. The party was still jumping, and the drinks were still coming . . . wait! Lydia recalled Dwight saying that he and Menage were best friends, so why on earth wasn't Menage here?

Scorpion looked through the scope sitting on top of the M-16.

He was hidden in a tree across the street from Dwight's condo, his back to the beach. "Come on, Dee-wi-tee," he said in a childlike voice, moving the crosshairs slowly to the left in search of his target.

"Hey, Dwight, I need to speak to you for a second," said Jamal walking up to him.

Dwight smiled and pointed at the lipstick on Jamal's cheek. "Yes, lover boy, what's up?" he asked with his back to the huge floor-to-ceiling window.

Scorpion saw Dwight and quickly zeroed the crosshairs in on the back of his head. One by one he would take out those who had messed up his plan, including Menage, Felix, Covington, and anyone else who got in his way.

"Yo, man, I got something you might want to see. Remember that chick, Latosha?"

Dwight cleared his throat. "Yeah, what about her?" He did his best to stay calm. Jamal reached into his pocket and pulled out the picture he had of Lydia, but it fell to the floor, along with his wallet and a condom. Dwight bent down to pick up the folded picture between his feet just as the glass window shattered behind him. All hell broke loose as he hit the floor. The bullet meant for him drilled Jamal just below his right eye, dropping him onto the leather couch.

"Fuck!" Scorpion cursed upon seeing the wrong target go down. His temper now lost, he unloaded the clip of the M-16 through the shattered window. Dwight crawled away from the window as round after round tore into his condo. One round hit the fishtank, sending gallons of water flooding into the den. Everybody panicked, and women were yelling at the top of their lungs, only to catch a stray bullet in the chest. Dwight looked up to see that one of his barbers had been hit twice in the back of the head after jumping on top of a woman. One man he didn't know lay spread out on his couch, bleeding from his stomach and shaking in a violent convulsion. "Tina!" Dwight yelled out. Rounds continued to tear into the walls before the bullets stopped.

"Everybody stay the fuck down!" Dwight yelled. "Tina . . . Tina!" There was yelling and crying, and the smell of human excrement was strong in the condo. Dwight reached for his gun, but it wasn't there. He had left it in his bedroom. *Damn, I'm slipping,* he thought. "Tina!"

Scorpion jumped from the tree and stumbled. He ran to the stolen Pathfinder and tossed the M-16 out the window. He opened the door and reached under the seat, finding what he needed to finish the job before the police showed up. Running back up the street, he laughed out loud like a child.

Lydia reached between her legs and pulled out a .380. She had dove behind the bar when the first shots were fired. She placed the back of her hand over her nose and mouth. The smell was unbearable. Kicking off her high heels, she eased toward the window with her back against the nearby wall. "Stay down!" she ordered a man about to stand. She hit the light switch and the room became dark. Men and women were moaning from fear and the sheer reality of death. Her heart was beating fast as she neared the shattered window that now allowed a gust of cool air from the sea to freshen the foul air in the condo. Stepping in something wet and soft, she willed herself to move on.

Scorpion was just about to pull the pin on the grenade and toss it through the dark window. Even with the lights out, the grenade would still have a deadly result.

Detective Covington was a block away when the call for shots fired came over the new radio in his Montero. He slid the truck to a halt when he saw a man in the middle of the street dressed in all black. "Freeze, police! Don't move! Hands in the air! Now!" he yelled standing in the door of the Montero and putting his Glock-45 in a death grip. Scorpion was about thirty yards away with his back to him. "Do it now!" Detective Covington yelled again. Where in the hell was his backup? He glanced at the shattered window of the condo and then at his suspect. He prayed that he wasn't some hit man Menage had hired. If he was, things could get messy, especially since DJ was at the party, which he had learned earlier.

Scorpion aimed the grenade at Covington and laughed hysterically. "Do you really want me to drop this, Dominique?" he asked.

Detective Covington squinted his eyes in the man's direction. His voice sounded so familiar. "Ham . . . Hamilton, is that you?" Covington asked slowly lowering his glock. "Hamilton, what the hell is going on here?" he asked stepping from behind the door.

"My name is Scorpion."

"What the . . . "

Scorpion, a.k.a. Detective Hamilton, spun around holding a Beretta and a barrage of black talon shells, the same ones he used to kill that smart-mouthed black kid. Detective Covington dove back into his SUV as glass rained down on top of him. The Beretta rang out in the street until the clip was empty. Lydia had been peeping out the window watching the entire scene. She assumed the man in the street shooting at the SUV was a cop until he turned sideways and reared back to toss an object. It took her a second to realize what he was about to do and she quickly aimed and fired her .380 as fast as she could. Hamilton released the object and she kept firing until her world went white, then black as she was tossed backward from the explosion of the grenade. A few pieces of hot shrapnel made its way into the condo. Detective Covington staggered out of his ruined Montero, only to see that the grenade had exploded the busted window of the condo. Seeing Hamilton or Scorpion run down the street to a parked SUV, he ran to the front of his vehicle, holding his Glock-45 in a two-handed shooter stance. Slowly taking a careful aim, his first shot shattered the back glass of the Pathfinder. Five more followed in rapid succession before the Pathfinder locked its brakes, slinging around the corner and out of sight. Pulling out his cell phone, Covington called dispatch, requested a medical team and gave the description of the Pathfinder as he jogged toward the condo, his .45 leading the way. In the distance he could hear the cavalry on its way. Slapping in a fresh clip, he approached the front door of the condo. "Miami Dade Police!" he yelled. "Coming in!"

Scorpion repeatedly slammed his head into the window as he turned out the lights on the Pathfinder and sat parked under a bridge back in Overtown. He stepped out of the truck and looked around the vacant lot at the uncut grass, rusted shopping carts, broken bottles, and hungry looking dogs. The smell of unwashed human bodies was strong, as there was a group of homeless people sitting nearby on crates watching his every move. Seeing he had no food or anything, they dissed him.

"Hey, how about y'all sleep in the truck here? There's food also," Scorpion said gesturing toward the Pathfinder.

"Thinks we's stupid, mister? We get in, den you call the po-po, huh! Go find somebody else ta fuck wif!" said a dingy looking man with a nappy matted beard.

Scorpion looked at the group of four men and what appeared to be a woman sitting in the middle wearing a faded tank top, her saggy breasts peeking out the side. She smiled at Scorpion, revealing her rotten teeth. "Only two dollars if you want some head," she said in a raspy voice.

Scorpion looked up as a truck roared across the bridge over head. It was dark since most of the street lamps were busted, and they would stay that way. This was one of the sections of Miami that remained in the dark for obvious reasons.

"I'll give you twenty if you sit in my truck until I get back."

The woman quickly stood up, but the man who had spoken first pushed her back down.

"I'll do it, mister," he said stumbling toward Scorpion with his hands reaching outward. Scorpion gave him the money and quickly turned to walk away.

"Crazy dude," the man muttered, getting into the Pathfinder. "Come on, fools, le's strip dis thang and leave." His crew didn't have to be asked twice. They thought that maybe they could jack the radio and get some wine. Scorpion stopped and looked back after getting a block and a half away and saw four figures running to the Pathfinder. He knew they would rummage the truck for any opportunity to steal, and they would pay extra attention to the bag in the back seat. It was worthless, but deadly. Once moved, it would release the clip on the grenade that was wedged between the seat. Suddenly there was a loud crack as the grenade exploded, killing everyone inside, followed by a loud echo down the street. The explosion made a huge hole in the roof of the truck, leaving it nearly topless.

"I'll do it, mister," Scorpion said playfully in that chilling childlike voice. He turned and made his way down the darkened road, disappearing under the next broken street lamp.

The first three ambulances hit their lights and sirens to clear a path and headed to Jackson Memorial. Five more lined the street as paramedics rushed back and forth from the condo.

Countless Miami Dade police cars blocked off the street. The total body count was now at nine, a few wounded and all scared shitless. Detective Covington sat on the hood of his Montero smoking a Newport as he watched another body being brought out in a bag. Everyone looked up when the Med-Vac helicopter flew overhead with its lights flashing before landing on the nearby beach. Detective Covington still couldn't believe that his partner was Scorpion, and he had no clue what the hell was going on. He thought about that helicopter crashing at sea, and his side kick being nowhere around. So who or what was Detective Hamilton? Covington wanted answers and he wanted them now!

"Covington, what the hell happened here?" asked FBI agent Todd Davis. "I heard that a fully automatic weapon and some explosives were used . . . thought I'd lend a hand." Covington flicked his Newport in the gutter and told him what had gone down. "Wait!" Agent Davis said holding up his hand. "Did you just say that Detective Hamilton is Scorpion?" Agent Davis was with the team of FBI agents that had closed in on the traced call to the hotel in Homestead. He had watched two of his men die in a split second after being exposed to C4. He thought

Scorpion was dead, killed in the helicopter that was shot down at sea. FBI agent, Neil Lofton, had told him that it was all over, but from the looks of the scene in front of him, he had no doubt that he was looking at the work of Scorpion. Agent Davis knew Detective Hamilton. They had run into each other a few times playing racquetball.

"What is it, Todd? Do you know something?" asked Covington with agitation.

"I need to make a call," said Agent Davis.

"I'm sorry, man, but this is now a federal case," said Davis. He knew Detective Covington wasn't going to like it, but it was over his head.

"You know that's bullshit, now don't cha?" Covington said with a deep sigh. Even as they talked, federal agents started pulling up and taking over the scene. "So who in the hell is Detective Hamilton? Can you at least tell me that?"

"Man, trust me on this one. It goes all the way to D.C. and I can't say anymore, but it's big," Agent Davis said shrugging his shoulders. Covington lit another Newport and deeply inhaled. "Covington, don't get any ideas, because even if you catch Sco-I mean, Detective Hamilton, the feds will pull

him from you before you even take his mug shot."
Agent Davis knew the Hostage Rescue Team was
about to hit the scene. "And I'd advise you not to
get in the way because . . . just go home, okay? And
take my word on this one," he said.

Covington nodded his head and started yelling out to his men to let the feds have it. Most
of them were happy about the news. He stopped
at the back of an ambulance as the paramedics
worked over a body. Blood was everywhere.
What caught his attention was a woman in an
iridescent top soaked with blood, pleading with
the paramedics to save her fiancé. From years of
experience, he knew the sound of a body about
to flatline. The woman fell back against the
wall, letting out an animal-like wail as the doors
closed. Her fiancé was dead.

Covington caught a ride back to the station
with another detective. He needed to think
things through. Truth be told, he was shook. The
FBI, D.C., what the fuck! He hadn't even called
Menage, and there was no telling where DJ was.
Everything seemed to be moving at a dizzying
pace, and before Covington had been able to get
a good look at all the bodies, the feds appeared
and took over.

***

Dough-Low and Menage sat in the living-room of Kamesa's apartment watching Martin Lawrence's standup act in *Runteldat* on DVD. Kamesa and Sherika went out to Burger King to buy some food. Menage looked down at his Bulova. It was one forty.

"Yo, Dough?"

"Yeah?"

"Do you ever think about how we be killing our own kind and shit? I bet them hate groups could retire. And I know I ain't no saint, either. Hell, I remember standing on the corner for you when I was in the fourth grade, yelling out when nine was rolling through. But I just been looking at this shit. Ain't no niggas slanging on the corner in the white part of town. Ain't no corner liquor stores, no porn shops, none of that shit. Now you know I'm not raggin' on you, 'cause you do your thing. Shit, I'm breaking the law, too, but we killed three of our own, and Dough, this shit ain't right, man. And we can speak from both sides because we saw how it was in the Beans. Instead of having a park to play in, all we had was bullet shells and buckets to beat on, milk crate basketball hoops, pissy mattresses acting like we was in the WWF and shit." He glanced over at Dough-Low, who was laid back in his brown Lazy Boy, sipping on a bottle of Perrier.

"You telling the truth. Ain't nobody forced me to slang. But a muthafucka sure as hell wasn't gonna give me no job with a felony, and I had to put food on the table. Had to do what I had to do. This shit ain't glamorous, but it's all I got. You think I like lookin' over my shoulder every damn day, wondering if some nigga I shot or stuck up is waitin' to catch me slippin'? Huh? Fuck no, but you know the saying, you gotta lay in the bed you made." Dough-Low finished his water. "No matter how much paper you make, you can't change the world, Menage. Tell you the truth, if I could, I'd give all this shit up and be out with Kamesa and say fuck all this bullshit. Oh, it's true! People of our kind get their foot in the door sometimes. Look at Sherika. The bitch is paid, nigga, and she ain't need no man to get hers, ain't sellin' no ass or nothing, so I'm not gonna sit here and say the white man holdin' me down."

"Yeah, I feel ya. But the whole setup is bullshit, man."

"Nigga, it's been this way since we were slaves!" Dough-Low said turning down the TV. "What about how we knock up our own women then leave 'em to raise the kids by their damn selves? I hate seein' that shit, but that's how it is, Menage. You want me to lay my guns down?"

"No."

"If DJ walked through that door right now, what would you do?"

"I'd—"

"You would smoke his bitch ass without a thought, just like you did that dude at Bayside. Now there's your black on black. Niggas see how it's going down but they, I mean we, keep doing the same fuckin' shit. And then these silly bitches won't fuck wit' a nigga if he trying to do right. They laugh at a nigga workin' at BK or Subway, but they quick to latch onto a nigga slangin' that dope. Why? 'Cause dem dumb bitches' brains are all fucked up. And you know I'm tellin' the truth. And it's cool to get shot or to have a record. Back when I started in the game, I did it 'cause I had to. Nowadays these fools do it just to cop some ice. Yeah, I see what's going on and I know it's fucked up. If you wasn't my nigga, I wouldn't even be having this conversation with you, but we came up in the hood together and you know how it is . . . and how the Ds be on me."

"So I guess Nas said it right," said Menage.

"Life's a bitch and then ya die. And speakin' of gettin' high, what's up, or have you gone and got religious on me?" Dough-Low said turning the TV volume back up. "But I told you Sherika was straight. Did she give you any dome?" he added.

Menage started grinning and then shook his head. He was about to light up a blunt but his phone chimed. He knew it was a female by the sexy tone. "Holla."

"Hey, boy, what are you doing up so late?"

"Hey, what's up Passion?" he asked leaning back on the couch.

"Mmm, you sound happy to hear from me. Am I right?"

"Yeah. What's up wit' you?" Menage felt good hearing her sweet voice.

"Sneaking on the phone; my girl . . . girlfriend had to take her brother to work and to be honest, I've been thinking about you a lot. I had to wait till she left . . . I just needed to hear your voice."

"Well, I'm glad you called. Are you doing okay?"

"Yes and no," she said.

"Talk to me then."

"Menage, I really been thinking of you a lot, even when I'm with her. You made me realize that all men ain't the same, and I thank you for that."

"It's no big deal."

"Yes, Menage, it is a big deal. I know you didn't come back for me. You came back for your phone, but I know that every thing you did after that you did because you wanted to. And I just need to know if you still respect me because—"

"Yes, I respect you, Passion. Now just listen to me, okay?"

"Okay."

"Girl, I can't judge you from one night of sex. I used to tell myself that a woman ain't shit if she fuck on the first day because there's no telling how many other times she's done it. But I wanted you, Passion, and circumstances brought us together, not lust. I can't sit here and lie and say I don't wanna see you again, and not just to get you in bed. I wanna spend some time with you and get to know you better. My life ain't all perfect and my past ain't clean, so don't be so down on yourself."

Passion was silent for a few seconds. "Menage, I need to get my life together. I'm up here kissing another woman thinking of you. Even when we like, uh, do our thing, I'm thinking of you. I need someone to put me first and not beat on me because I'm not perfect."

"Come back, Passion," he said meaning every word.

"I . . . I don't know, Menage. Please understand that I need to take my time with this."

"Take your time, but remember that I still respect you."

"Do you miss me?"

"Yes, I do."

"Que desea usted?"

"Huh?"

"Boy, that's Spanish for what do you wish?" She giggled.

"So you speak Spanish, huh?" he asked wishing he could see her smile.

"Yes."

"Well, I wish that you do whatever makes you happy, even if it's not with me."

"Menage, look, Trish is pulling up, so I have to go."

"Passion?"

"Yes."

"I still respect you, okay?"

"I know you do, Menage. Trust me, I know." "You take care, okay special?"

"Special what?"

"You, you're special to me, so take care."

"Menage . . . " He could hear her voice starting to quiver.

"Baby, just call me later, okay? You don't need no beef with your, uh, girl. I'll be here for you, okay? So give me a kiss and be easy, baby."

"Okay," she said softly, and uttered something else in Spanish.

"Passion, I don't . . ." He paused then added, "Just keep your eyes dry and your heart easy."

"I love you, Menage. Please understand that I need time." She had translated what she knew he hadn't understood. Then she hung up before he could reply. He closed the phone slowly and gently tapped it against his forehead.

"You straight, dog?" Dough-Low asked.

"Yeah. Remember them two chicks at the park when you fucked that dude up wit' the jammed heater?"

"Yeah."

"Well, that was the shorter one."

"What . . . you mean you smashing his girl? Damn, I know you had a field day with that phat booty." Dough-Low cut his conversation short and stood up when Kamesa and Sherika came in with the food. "'Bout fuckin' time," he said rubbing his stomach.

"Fool, please!" Kamesa said heading for the kitchen. "If your tail was so hungry, you should've went your damn self. Go out to the car and get those bags. I stopped at the twenty-four-hour food market."

After the four ate, Menage found himself sitting alone on the couch with Sherika. A second round of sex looked promising, but his Nokia vibrating on his hip put that on pause. After a short conversation, he ended the call and told Sherika that he had to tend to some business but promised to get up with her later. He pulled up to his shop around two thirty and found Tony sitting in his blood red Ford Supercrew F-150 with tinted windows.

"What's up?" Menage asked when he came to a stop next to Tony's Ford.

"Remember my cousin I told you about who works at Paul's Toyota? She got copies for three Landcruisers fresh off the truck last week."

"Will they look at her if they come up missing?"

"Hell no. She messes around with one of the salesmen and she's been there for a while."

Menage looked up at Tony and smiled. "Tell her I'll give her ten Gs for the three keys."

Tony would still get his cut once the three SUVs were tagged and sold. His cousin would be more than happy to take ten thousand for three minutes of work.

"And give her the whole amount, Tony." Coming off ten thousand would bring him back close to ninety grand, having the three brand new Landcruisers on the market well under the fifty thousand dollar price tag.

"Hey, boss, why you ain't at the party?" Tony asked lighting up a Newport.

"What party?"

"Tina and Dwight's."

"Ain't heard nothin' 'bout no party," Menage said.

"Well, my girl got a call and told me about it. But she didn't go. Don't like Tina that much."

Menage shrugged his shoulders. "I'll ask Dwight about it tomorrow. Anyway, go ahead and get Kayvon, Alex, and Ace to pick up the Landcruisers. I think I know a dude up in Tampa that might buy two of 'em."

They tied up the business and drove their separate ways. Driving back to his mansion was a quick and silent trip for Menage. Maybe Tony had heard wrong. Why would Dwight have a party and not invite him? Vapor met him before he got out of his car. Leaving half the lights out, he moved toward the kitchen to grab a bottle of Colt 45. It was late and he was thinking of Latosha. He wanted to see her and talk to her. Maybe things would be different with her, he thought. Maybe Latosha would fill the void that Chandra had left. Ignoring the time, he dialed her number as he fell onto his couch. After the tenth ring he hung up. Benita's number now glowed under his thumb, but again he thought of Latosha. She meant something to him more than just sex. He wanted to laugh at himself for being a sucker for love. He tried Latosha's number again. A smile appeared on his face when he heard the phone being answered after the fourth ring, but it quickly faded when the male voice on the other end caused him to sit up. Vapor's attention was on Menage now, sensing his mood yet again. Menage almost dropped the beer as the news filled his ear. Jumping to his feet, he rushed outside with Vapor on his heels. Everything seemed to stand still as the blood rushed to his head. Vapor backed up as Menage mounted his Suzuki 1300-R Hayabusa. Smoking the back wheel, he shot through the gate, hoping to beat the time.

On I-95 with his feet up on the back pegs tucked under the windscreen, he ignored his speed, which was approaching 180 miles per hour. Dr. Wilson had to be wrong. He prayed that he was wrong as he neared the hospital. The tears streamed down his face behind the tinted shield of his helmet. The Hayabusa moved swiftly as if on air, causing the cars he passed to appear motionless. *Maybe if I was there,* he thought to himself. Menage roared toward the hospital's front entrance, locking the back wheel of his bike and causing the few people on the scene to scatter. The bike crashed on its side, snapping the rearview mirror as he dropped it, running for the entrance of the hospital. Reaching the front desk, he struggled to yank the helmet off as a nurse asked him to calm down. The helmet fell to the floor with a sharp crack, followed by

Menage yelling for a room number. Once he got it, he took off running, ignoring an officer asking him to slow down.

Taking the stairs, he reached the fourth floor, breathing heavily and sped up as he saw Dr. Wilson standing in the hall. Upon seeing Menage, he motioned for him to follow. They moved quickly toward the room. Dr. Wilson immediately told him of his patient's injuries, shrapnel to the face and chest with internal bleeding that couldn't be stopped.

Menage was already in tears when Dr. Wilson closed the door behind him, leaving him alone with her. She weakly called out his name as he neared the bed. Since the lights were low, he was unable to see the full damage to the once beautiful face. He moved to her side and took her hand. He started to speak but she told him who she was, stunning him. She asked him to forgive her. "Yes, Lydia," he said, the tears rolling down his face. "I won't let you go, baby, so just relax 'cause it's gonna be all right. I promise I won't leave you, okay," he said doing his best to keep from breaking down.

"Re-remember our song?" she asked faintly.

"Yeah, I still got your CD. I'ma give it back to you when I take you up outta here." The tears continued to run freely down his face.

"T-tell me how it w-would have been with us."

He sniffed hard, trying to be stronger for her. He had already lost Chandra, but losing Lydia he wasn't prepared to do. "How about I tell you how it's *going* to be. It's gonna be you, me, and Vapor. We can move to anyplace you want in this world."

She squeezed his hand. "Stay out of trouble for me," she said in a low whisper. He could hear her getting weaker. "And know that . . . that I really did care for you, Menage, and I didn't want it to end like this." She squeezed his hand again.

"Shhhh, baby girl. Ain't nothing gonna end, you hear me?" Lydia's lips began to quiver, and Menage kissed her gently. Lydia fought her hardest to return the kiss, but she couldn't .

"Please fight this, Lydia, 'cause I swear I need you, girl." His tears came pouring down again. *If love is real, she'll live,* he thought.

"Menage?"

"Yeah, baby, I'm still here."

"I got another song I want you to listen to." He looked around for a radio but didn't see one. She slid her gown to one side, exposing her stomach. "Kiss me again," she said. Menage kissed her, and she laid his head near her heart. She lightly caressed his neck and told him that she loved him. "Listen to that song inside of me. It's called true love, Menage." She struggled to form a smile.

He knew she wouldn't make it, but she deserved to live. He wanted her to live. He closed his eyes, enjoying her soft touch, knowing that she was alive as long as his head rose up and down with the rhythm of her stomach and the beating of her heart. There was no song that could compare to this and he never wanted it to end. But suddenly the song was over. Menage felt her take her last breath. There were no parting words or wishes or doctors rushing into the room. Lydia Nansteel died loving Menage Unique Legend. He burst into tears, soaking the hospital gown. "Be strong, nigga," he told himself, but his efforts were futile. Kissing her one last time he left the dark room, realizing why she had wanted the lights off. She wanted him to remember her beautiful face and not the one torn apart by some shrapnel . . . Every time there was love there came pain.

Walking down the hall, he could feel all of his emotions building up inside of him until it became physically unbearable. He ran to the restroom and emptied his stomach. He cleaned himself up and looked in the mirror.

Menage looked at his surroundings. Although the bathroom was far from spotless, he admitted to himself it was far cleaner than his life. He was tired, soul tired. Stepping back out into the hallway, he saw a woman backing out of a room across the hall in tears and realized that he wasn't the only one in pain. He lowered his head and began to reflect on the recent events of his life as he heard someone call his name. He looked up and saw Tina staggering toward him with makeup smeared all over her face and blood on her clothes.

"Menage, Dwight's dead," she said over and over. His mouth dropped open as Tina fell into his arms. Too stunned to speak, he automatically embraced her.

The night was far from over. Dwight's condo was off limits until the FBI could fully go over the scene. They knew about Scorpion and he was all they wanted. The reason Scorpion had targeted the condo wasn't really all that deep. That's what the FBI had gotten from the CIA.

Two FBI agents sat in a tinted Suburban across the street from the condo. The loud explosion shocked them both, the blast sending spider webs on all the windows. Both agents staggered out of the Suburban holding their heads. The driver pulled out his weapon on GP as his passenger called for backup. For the second time, the street was filled with flashing lights and federal agents.

Half a block away, Detective Covington looked at his watch as he sat in a green Shelby Dodge Durango. It was after four in the morning. When two men dressed in black got into the truck, he quickly pulled away from the curb, making a U-turn. He had no choice but to destroy the condo for fear of any evidence being in there that could point to his Uncle Felix. He had called Menage and told him about the DB-7 as well as the possibility of Scorpion still being alive. Covington realized that Menage was probably in shock, and he was certain that he was when Menage told him that Tina, who was in shock as well, was with him. And as for DJ . . . not a soul knew where he was.

Chapter 8

Clocks Everywhere!

Just three days later, Menage watched two special people get buried who didn't need to die. These days, Tina was with him, but it was as if she wasn't really there. He didn't even bother to try talking to her. All she did was stay in one of his bedrooms crying.

Menage lay in his bedroom looking up at the ceiling. Scorpion had vanished, but deep down he knew he would show his face again. He also knew that Tina had no clue of the pictures or tape he had. So what, DJ had winked at her; did that mean anything? So what she was fucking around on Dwight. He had done the same thing to Chandra.

He hated that he had a conscience. He felt sorry for Tina. He remembered the first night when he stood at her closed door with the pictures, and how hearing her crying had stopped him from taking another step. He was supposed to kick her ass out onto the street, but he couldn't. Dwight died loving that woman.

Menage had been avoiding Benita since Lydia died. He hadn't touched a woman since. His bedroom was semidark and silent, Glock-19 resting on his stomach, hands behind his head. The chop shop was shut down, but he now had full control of the four MD Beauty salons, so money was not a problem.

Anger began to boil in his stomach as he thought of Tina. The Lexus, BMW, and Viper were being sold. Those sales alone would give her close to $150,000, and he didn't even want to give her that. If it weren't for Dwight he'd do nothing, but deep down he knew he had a weakness for anyone in pain. If Dough-Low was in his shoes, Tina would be in bad shape or maybe even dead. But he wasn't Dough-Low. He was Menage Unique Legend.

He had loved Chandra, hadn't he? But yet he cheated on her, so how was he any different from Tina? He hated her even more because he saw himself in her. He felt like shit. His mind was made up. He'd give her the money from the cars and a few grand and send her on her way. And as for Dwight's mill, he'd already had it switched to his account. If Tina had any beef he'd toss the pictures of she and DJ in her face and tell her to charge it to the game. Now that made him feel better. He smiled just thinking of the look that would be on her face.

Putting on a pair of cotton FUBU jogging pants, he picked up the pictures of DJ and Tina and headed for his elevator. He went to the room where she was staying. The door was cracked. He was about to push it open but he stopped when he saw Tina stepping out of the bathroom. He could tell she had been crying by her puffy eyes. Her hair was wrapped up in a turban style with another towel. He watched her dry off her thick thighs and saw the way her ass moved each time she made the slightest gesture. She stood sideways now, and her full breasts swayed back and forth as she bent forward. As she dried between her legs, he realized that he was getting turned on. The sun beaming on his neck and back wasn't the only thing getting warmer. Tina took the towel off her head, and Menage was about to move when he saw her remove the large towel from her body and place it over her face. She stood facing him now with her legs parted, giving him a full frontal view of her well-stacked body. She dropped the towel to the floor and reached into a bag that sat on the bed. She then rubbed some scented oil all over her body. Just as she was snapping her bra, Menage knocked at the door. She threw on a pair of panties and a T-shirt that stopped right below her ass. She picked the towel up off the floor and sat on the bed.

"It's open, Menage," she said looking down at her pedicured toes.

"W-we need to talk, Tina, and I think we should do it now," Menage said sitting at the edge of the bed beside her. "I'ma give you a chance to come clean about anything that I should know about, and ain't no need for no tears," he added. Tina's lips started to quiver.

"About what?" she asked nervously, not knowing how much he really knew.

"About DJ and about these marks on my chest . . . and Bayside," he said keeping his cool.

"He made me do it, Menage, I swear," Tina said, her voice cracking.

"Do what, Tina?" he snapped.

Still looking at her feet, Tina took a deep breath. "DJ . . . he and I were seeing each other behind Dwight's back and he came to trust me. And after you were shot and in a coma, I went to see him while Dwight was visiting Felix. That night he told me that he had put the two hits on you. I guess he figured I wouldn't care, but I did. We started to fuss and he told me if I said anything about it, he'd send Dwight a tape of us having sex or do what he did to you to Dwight or me," she lied.

Menage sighed. The pictures meant nothing now since she confessed that she was fucking DJ, and the night she mentioned, when Dwight was visiting Felix, was the night the pictures were taken.

"When the last time you seen DJ?" he asked ignoring her tears.

"At the party," Tina said, finally looking at Menage.

"The party I didn't know about!"

"I told Akissi to call you. She was the one who made all the calls for me. And Dwight didn't even know about it until a few hours before. Everyone figured you didn't want to come." Since Akissi was killed, Tina's lie was as good as gold.

"I thought you loved Dwight! He gave you the world, Tina. How could you do that to him?"

"Think of how Chandra loved you and how you—"

"Leave her out of this, Tina!" he said seeing the fear in her eyes. His fists were balled up, but he knew damn well he wouldn't hit her.

"Menage, I'm sorry. I didn't know what to do. Please believe me," she cried.

"Do you have any money stashed away?" She shook her head no, another lie. "I'll see what I can do for you. The feds cleared Dwight's account," he lied.

"What about DJ? What are we going to do about him? I'm scared, Menage," she said wrapping her arms around herself, slowly rocking from side to side.

"You'll be fine with me. Don't you have family somewhere up north?"

"I got a cousin in Richmond, Virginia."

Menage lay back on the bed and stared at the ceiling. "Tina, I always looked at you and Dwight with envy," he said softly.

"Why?" she asked, looking at him over her shoulder.

"Because I figured he had life all figured out and because he had you in his corner. Before meeting Chandra, I used to try to find a woman like you, someone I could trust and commit to. But you made me realize that love ain't shit but a fake-ass, four letter word."

Tina swung her legs onto the bed and lay sideways, resting on her elbow. "That's not true, Menage," she whispered.

"Yeah, right!" he said, his forearm resting across his closed eyes.

"So you don't hate me?"

"Why should I? 'Cause you like sex like I do? Nah. We just two fools who didn't realize true love when it was dead in our faces." His eyes remained closed when he heard Tina break into tears. Maybe she was right. He felt her weight shift on the bed. He moved his arm from over his eyes just in time to see her straddle his waist. Her shirt was off, and he couldn't help but look at the roundness of her breasts showing under her bra. He stared into her tear-filled eyes. "This ain't right, Tina," he said. She ignored him as she slid her hands across his stomach and over his chest. She massaged his chest and felt his heart pounding.

"I'm going to miss him, Menage, really I am. I know I cheated on him and did things I'll forever regret, but my love was real. I swear I loved him."

"Loved or *love,* Tina?" he asked. She turned her head to the side and wiped her face with the back of her hand.

Menage realized he had the same kind of feelings for Chandra that Tina had for Dwight. Tina didn't answer his question. Instead she continued to rub his chest. "Why did you take away my sunshine?" she asked, knowing he was enjoying her touch. She felt his throbbing erection underneath her.

"What are you talking about?" She glanced over her shoulder at the ray of sunlight on the floor, beaming through the cracked door. Menage now realized she knew he had been standing at the door, blocking the sunshine. He sucked his teeth then let out a deep breath. "Get up, Tina. Let's stop before—"

"Before what?" she asked reaching around to unhook her bra, taking it off slowly. He started to push her off of him but she reached for his wrists, placing his hands on her oily breasts. When she let go of his wrists, his hands remained where they were. Menage moved his hands down her soft body and she closed her eyes. She then leaned forward and took off her panties.

"Stop, Tina, we don't need to be doing this," Menage said running his hands up and down her back. He felt her twitch when he slid a finger between her ass cheeks , and he lifted his torso as she pulled down his pants. Menage wore no boxers, and they were now both naked.

"I hated you so much, Menage," she said looking into his eyes. He could feel the heat from her sex as her pubic hairs brushed against his penis. She reached down to grab his dick, and that's as far as things got before he stopped her.

Minutes later, Tina was pulling out of the driveway in Dwight's Bentley, and that was the last time Menage saw her. She was going to Virgina lonely and with the exact value in cash from the cars that she and Dwight owned. Menage knew she probably had a stash hidden someplace, so he didn't give her a penny more. The main thing was that she was out of his life.

Dough-Low later pulled up in his Hummer H2. He was in the living room blowing on the pit bull chamber of his gun while Menage was upstairs taking a shower. Menage had told him to be on the lookout for a cop who Detective Covington was sending over to keep an eye on things.

Menage stood in the shower thinking of how close he had come to fucking Tina. He blamed it on all the stress she was under after losing Dwight, but he knew that wasn't true. And sure, he wanted her, but for once he didn't allow lust and his weakness for the flesh to rule over him. And he actually felt good about it. An hour of good, toe-curling sex and a lifetime of guilt just weren't worth it.

"Damn, Dwight, why it had to be you? Me and my crazy world," he said to himself as he thought of Lydia and the last song she played for him.

***

Scorpion was stretched out naked in bed with another prostitute in an hourly-rate hotel in Overtown. He replayed the tape in a small device that was hooked up to a pair of head-phones he wore. He had just heard a coversa-tion between Detective Covington and Menage as a result of bugging Detective Covington's phone.

"What are you listening to?" the red-haired prostitute asked. She knew Scorpion didn't have it all. But for four hundred she didn't complain when all he had to pay was twenty. Scorpion took off the headphones and told her to shut up and get on her back. "Anything you say, big boy," she said spreading her legs wide for him. "It's all yours." He mounted her quickly. "Ugh . . . easy, big boy, we got all day . . . ah, yes, that's the spot." She tried to get him to show some kind of emotion, but he was in another world. "Is it good to you? Ugh . . . ah . . ." Well, if he wasn't going to enjoy himself, she sure as hell would. Her pale breasts jerked wildly as he drove in and out of her. The headboard hit the wall above her head repeatedly. Four hundred bucks for what? An hour of mind-blowing sex. Cupping her own juicy breasts and wrapping her lanky legs around his thrusting hips, she realized that this man had never stopped to put on a condom. But what difference did it make? She already had HIV. "Do it, big boy, cum in my love hole," she said with her eyes closed. She felt his weight shift on top of her as he kept pumping. Keeping her eyes closed, she let her body enjoy the release that she desired so desperately. And she felt no guilt whatsoever passing along her virus.

"Taste it," Scorpion said with no emotion as he continued to pound into her steadily.

"Mmm . . . s-say what, baby?" She opened her eyes just in time to see an odd-looking black object coming toward her face. Scorpion shoved the Beretta into her mouth, splitting her lip and knocking out a few of her front teeth. Blood spilled out of her mouth, and before she could react he pulled the trigger, blowing her brains out. Collapsing on top of her, he continued to thrust until he came deep inside of her. "Thank you, thank you," he uttered as the juices flowed from his loins into her dead body.

Across the hall, the dead prostitute's friend was on her knees, pleasing her john when she heard the shot. Ignoring the man's swearing when she took his penis out of her mouth, she rushed to the phone and called the police. Since they were in the run down area of Overtown, the police took their sweet time getting there. Scorpion was fully dressed when he heard the sirens. Peeking out the dirty curtain, he watched four officers heading toward the hotel as they crossed the street. Cracking his door moments later, he saw the officers slowly making their way toward his room with their guns drawn. "Childs play," he hissed. He placed his gun by the table near the door. Pulling out his only flash-bang grenade, he pulled the pin, counted to two and then flung the door open, tossing out the grenade in the path of the four officers. It went off with a deafening bang and a bright flash of light, intensifying the small hallway. The officers all fell to their knees, covering their heads and ears. Only one of them managed to hold onto his gun. Scorpion smoothly stepped out into the hallway with his Beretta and fired four perfect shots from a distance of thirty feet, killing each one instantly. By the time backup arrived, he was long gone.

More than fourteen officers crowded the hall in response to the call about their fellow officers being down. The head officer led his men, following the blood trail on the third floor to a vacant room. If they knew anything about Scorpion, they would have never kicked in the door. The entire four-story shabby hotel shook as the C4 was released. Glass rained down on the police officers still on the street. Smoke billowed from the third floor, thick and grey. All hell had broken loose.

Minutes later, two Blackhawk helicopters circled above the smoking building. "He was here!" yelled CIA field agent, Stanley Walters. "I can smell him! Take me down. I need a closer look. Have team two stay in the air!" he yelled even louder over the roar of the Blackhawk. When he hit the ground he approached agent Todd Davis, who stood next to a fire truck. "Was it our man?" Walters asked already knowing the answer. Davis told him about the prostitute who made the first call. She and the front desk clerk recognized the picture of Scorpion.

"How many dead?" Walters asked.

"Ten, so far. A few had to be taken out on a chopper. As soon as it's clear to enter the hotel, I'm going to see what's left," said Davis.

Walters ran his hand through his hair and let out a deep sigh. "Gonna be a long fucking day!" Once they got the okay sign, the FBI flooded the hotel.

Menage stood in his driveway with Lou, checking out his new Titanium colored Lamborghini

Murcielago 6.2. Dough-Low was inside cleaning his pistol. Menage wore a pair of baggy cotton Rocawear jogging pants and roll down Avirex boots. His custom made holster was wrapped around his neck, holding his Glock-19 under his right arm; it was too hot for a shirt. Vapor was running around the front yard chasing Dough-Low's red-nosed Pit, Chamber.

"When you gonna shoot the video for your new single?" Menage asked leaning on the hood of his Escalade.

"Next month. My manager 'posed to block off Sixty-second for a few hours. We can have the entire car club reppin', ya know!" Lou said sitting on the fender of his Lamborghini with the driver's side door up in the air, parked in front of Menage's Escalade. "Hey, yo, I talked to Big Chubb and he said he'll have a few dancers to spare. My man had a bachelor party a few days ago, and this bad chick with a phat ass and big tits was there . . . Benita, I think that was her name."

"Word?" Menage asked, wondering why in the hell his stomach started to turn.

"Yeah. Anyway, I think the boys ran a train on her, and this Hindu chick was there too."

Bitch, Menage thought, thinking how Benita had confessed her so-called love for him. Little did Lou know, while he was in the bathroom getting head from a groupie, Benita had left as soon as her job was over. The Hindu dancer was the one who had taken on the guys two and three at a time. The whole thing was even filmed. Menage had heard enough. *Fuck the bitch. Find 'em, fuck 'em and flee. Ain't no love.*

Dough-Low was inside looking out the window and saw what looked to be a cop walking across the street. He remembered the call from Detective Covington. Maybe he had something to tell Menage. The back of Lou's Lambo was facing the gate and Menage didn't see him approaching. Scorpion, dressed in a Miami Dade police uniform, approached the gate. He saw Menage leaning on the front of his SUV, but the door of the Lambo blocked his vision. Not only had he stripped one of the officers of his uniform, but he had stripped him of his two Glock-45s.

The sharp, loud cracking noise sent Lou and Menage to the ground. Pulling out his Glock-19, Menage fired blindly over his shoulder at the gate while seeking cover behind his SUV. Lou had somehow made his *way* beside Dough-Low's Hummer H2. Out of ammo, he *sat* on the ground with his head between his knees. Dough-Low, who was now on the scene, had let off a few rounds from his gun. Menage saw Dough-Low looking his *way* and shaking his head. He, too, *was* out of ammo.

The front windshield of the Escalade shattered as Scorpion figured that they were all out of ammo. He was about to fire close to the ground, hoping to hit Menage under the SUV, when suddenly two dogs rushed the gate. He snatched his wrist back in time, but his glock fell through the gate. He extended his arm to retrieve it and Vapor's fangs clenched his wrist. He tried to pull his wrist free, but Vapor's grip was too strong. Chamber even fought to get a piece of him. The dogs let out haunting growls, causing Scorpion further trauma. Pulling out his mace, he emptied the can and his bloody wrist was let loose. Both 45s lay on the other side of the gate. With no gun in hand, he rushed toward the stolen red Ferrari 360 Modena F-1. Menage rushed to the gate and saw the Ferrari speed off.

"Yo, Dough, call Covington and tell him what happened!" Menage yelled as he jumped into Lou's Murcielago.

"Hey, yo, man . . ." Lou said as Menage brought the door down.

"Watch out, nigga, watch out!" Menage said pushing Lou's hands away. Lou stood in the driveway with his hands on his hips as Menage threw the Murcielago in reverse. Smoking the tires, he rocketed through the gate as it slid open. Slamming on the brakes, straightening the car up and putting it into first, it shot forward with its backend chirping. Menage quickly shifted gears.

Scorpion was weaving through traffic in the Modena, ignoring the blowing horns and cars slamming on brakes as he cut off their pathway. He slid the Modena around a corner and fish tailed, nearly losing control. Wrong turn. He shifted in reverse, smoking the tires. Menage weaved through the thick traffic and thought he had lost the Modena until it whizzed through the intersection up ahead in reverse. Both cars sped toward the highway as if there was no rush hour traffic.

All hell broke loose when Detective Covington got the call. He knew it was out of his hands, and he quickly called FBI agent, Todd Davis. They didn't know if it was Scorpion or not, but who else would do something like this? A daytime hit, and drive off in a Ferrari? There was only one way to find out. Again the two Blackhawks took to the sky as word leaked out that the man suspected of killing a number of fellow officers of the Miami Police department had shown his face. A countywide APB was put out to catch a cop killer driving a red Ferrari. It didn't take long for a Metro Dade Police helicopter to spot the vehicle one mile from I-95.

Scorpion slammed on the brakes and ordered a sexy blonde wearing a tight miniskirt to get into the car. She saw the uniform and took a step back.

"Miss, I'm sure you heard about the . . . women being killed," he said referring to the prostitutes he had murdered. "It's urgent that you come with me. It's for your safety."

"Uh . . . where's your police car?"

"Look, we'll discuss that later! Trust me, we don't have much time." She shrugged her slender shoulders. After all, he was the police.

Sitting next to Scorpion, she noticed his bloody hand, and before she could ask him about it he knocked her out cold. Fortunately, for Scorpion's sake, the windows were tinted. He pulled from the curb with his hostage.

Menage slammed on the brakes, simultaneously putting the Murcielago in neutral as it made a full spin in a hail of smoke and squealing tires. He nearly missed the Ferrari taking the ramp toward I-95 North. Seconds later he hit the ramp and merged into the speeding traffic. Looking over his shoulder, he floored the Murcielago between two trucks as the rear spoiler popped up partially and the huge air ducks slid open. He shot forward, engine whining, zigzagging back and forth reaching over a hundred miles per hour. Scorpion saw the Murcielago gaining on him. Slapping the stitched leather steering wheel, he veered into the semiempty carpool lane and floored the Ferrari. Menage saw the Ferrari quickly accelerate. He gripped the steering wheel tightly. He slammed the gear in sixth, giving the car such a powerful kick that he felt as though he was hit from behind. He was up to 187 miles per hour in no time. Scorpion glanced in the mirror to see the Murcielago emerging from behind a slow moving car and veer back into the carpool lane. The Ferrari was outclassed. Pulling up three cars behind the Ferrari, Menage realized that he had no plan. He sure as hell wasn't going to cause a wreck at such a high speed, plus he had no ammo for his Glock-19 and Lou carried no heat.

The two cars sped on, crossing the Broward County line. As Scorpion came up on the next ramp, he saw a fuel truck slowly merging onto the I-95.

Reaching under the seat, he pulled out his Beretta and lowered the passenger's window. He knew he only had a few shots and one last chance. Gripping the wheel with his left hand, he waited for the perfect shot. From a distance of no more than a hundred yards, he opened up on the fuel truck. The loud wind and wailing engine drowned out the sounds of the shots, and his fourth shot hit the rig, causing it to explode in a loud, deafening roar as the Ferrari left the destruction in its path. Menage was going too fast to stop when the rig blew up, sliding sideways in the middle of the highway. Scorpion was laughing in that same childlike voice as he looked back at the burning rig, blocking half of I-95. Thick, black smoke billowed from the truck. He nearly lost control of the Ferrari when he saw the nimble Murcielago, now on fire as well, shoot from around the burning rig. The flames on the Murceilago were quickly put out from the rushing wind.

Menage fought to control the car as it skidded all over the road. Turning the wheel in the opposite direction of the back end, the tires squealed and locked just as the Murcielago made two full spins before coming to a stop inches from a family packed stationwagon that had stopped in the middle of the road. Menage let out a deep breath and dropped his forehead on the steering wheel just as a black helicopter roared overhead.

"Blue Two, this is Blue One!" yelled Stanley Walters, leading the way in the Blackhawk helicopter. "Suspect in sight up ahead. Looks like he's slowing down. We're on him. Stay back!"

Scorpion slowed the Ferrari in the thick traffic just as the Blackhawk roared overhead. He knew it was the CIA because the Blackhawk was a military aircraft.

CIA agent, Walters, leaned out the door of the Blackhawk holding a pair of high-powered binoculars. "He has a hostage. Can you disable the car without—" Before he could finish, one of the Hostage Rescue Team agents carrying a rifle sent two big balls of fire into the back of the Ferrari. Scorpion felt the car dying under him. Taking the next exit as the Blackhawk hovered behind him, he pointed the Beretta over his shoulder. Walters, not knowing that it wasn't loaded, quckly gained altitude and veered away for safety.

Scorpion pulled the smoking Modena into a small chain of department stores. He grabbed his hostage, now semiconscious, and put the gun to her head. He drove up to the closest store entrance as the Blackhawk helicopters hovered across the street. Scorpion smiled as he rushed through the entrance of Goines Guns and Ammo.

The two Blackhawks landed, and the HRT tactical agents quickly made their way across the street. It would take no more than ten minutes for CIA agent Walters to take full command of the problem, but since the CIA never really got the go ahead to move forward, he turned it over to FBI agent, Todd Davis. The road was blocked off, and four Broward County police helicopters hovered at a safe distance. The amount of Dade and Broward county police officers was close to one hundred.

"Okay, tell me what we got set up?" Walters asked kneeling next to the Hostage Rescue Team leader behind a four-foot-high brick wall.

"Sir, I got two agents covering the back door. Two on the roof, two under the truck to your right, two spaces from the gun shop, and the rest are behind me," said the team leader, his black-gloved hand gesturing energetically as he spoke. Walters peeked over his shoulder to see six HRT tactical agents kneeling down on one knee, holding deadly MP5s and wearing full assault gear. "Five hostages inside as we know, sir. We cleared out the bike shop next door. Actually, we cleared out the whole mini mall," added the team leader.

"Okay, good." Through his wire mic strapped to his Kevlar helmet, he heard FBI agent, Davis, ask if he wanted to use gas.

"No go!" Nine times out of ten there's tons of gas masks inside. Todd, make sure you keep a tight chain on the local police."

"Got it!"

"Scorpion's going down."

"The sooner the better."

Walters slowly peeked over the wall. Things looked peaceful. He spotted the hiding HRT tactical agents. "Your men ready?" he asked the team leader.

"On your word, sir."

"Well, I'll try to talk him out and if that doesn't work, I'm putting it in your hands. And yes, we'll employ the Rules of Engagement, shoot first and fuck the questions . . . dead men can't talk, huh?" The team leader only nodded his head in agreement.

Scorpion had killed the first man he came across in the gun shop. Everyone was caught off guard from his police uniform. Three men sat tied up on the floor. The sexy blonde, now fully conscious, was cuffed to the front door to stop or slow down entry from the HRT. Scorpion

was trained to survive, and that's exactly what
he had planned to do.

   Close to an hour had passed when Walters
got fed up. He was sweating like a pig. The black
suit he wore was drawing heat like dollars to a
G-string.
   "Pass me that bullhorn again." Fumbling with
the switch, he turned it on and gripped it.
   "Okay, Eugene, it's now or never. You know we
have you fully closed in, so let's bring this to an
end."
   The gun shop's glass window shattered. Heads
dropped as Scorpion let loose with an M-16.
Round after round tore into a police cruiser
parked behind Walters. "Everyone okay?"
Walters asked over the airwaves. Seconds later
everyone checked in, confirming their status.
"Looks like he doesn't want to talk. Take him
down!" Walters said turning it over to the HRT.
   "Heads up, heads up! Front door suspect coming out!" said one of the agents under the truck.
Suddenly the door swung open and Walters
looked up to see Scorpion stumble out, holding
a twelve gauge. A shot from somewhere set the
whole thing off.
   "Take him down!" yelled the team leader.
"Wait!" screamed Walters, a second too late.

The six HRT tactical agents rose up, resting their MPSs over the wall and opened fire, along with two under the truck. The quiet MPSs had a deadly result. It took a little while for some of the tactical agents to realize that their target wore a vest, and two direct hits finally tore through the black hood, drilling his forehead. He fell onto his back, never firing a shot nor dropping the shotgun. The two HRT agents from under the truck rushed toward his body, MPSs tucked under their chins. The team leader gave the order to cease fire, and the entire HRT held their weapons as cries of "Man down! Man down!" hit the airwaves.

"What the hell!" Walters said as the two agents on the roof gave the sign of a man being down in the back.

"Go, go, go around the back!" Walters yelled. The entire team rushed through the shop and came upon a body. The men on the roof were firing at something in the distance. All Walters heard was a motorcycle. "What in the hell is going on here!" he shrieked.

It didn't take long for them to realize that Scorpion had taped a gun to a hostage and pushed him out the front door, letting off a shot to get things started. He had done the same thing in the back. Coming back through the gun shop, they saw a hole in the wall leading to the motorcycle shop. The remaining hostages were all killed, gunshots to the head.

"What color was the bike?" Walters yelled running toward the Blackhawk.

"Red, sir . . . Honda 1100, I think."

"Fuck!" Walters hissed as he jumped into the Blackhawk, punching the copilot's seat. Seconds later, the Blackhawk rose from the ground and Walters called up Todd Davis. "Todd, make sure none of these local cops try to take him in."

"Might be hard."

"Hard my ass! Tell whoever goes against your rules that they will face a federal charge! They can only call in his position not detain him, and I mean it, Todd!"

"Relax. Broward has a full APB out and two of their choppers are still up, so it won't be long. I'ma take care of things down here, and Stanley . . ."

"Yeah!"

"It's getting messy." The two Blackhawks picked up the chase again.

Menage pulled up on Thunderboat row to check on the shipment of his speedboat. He had received a call from Detective Covington, telling him that Scorpion was still alive and they had him surrounded at a store in Broward County. He got out of the car and made his way into the large boat warehouse. Angel Falls was starting to creep into the back of his mind. Where else would he go? After making sure everything was in order with his speedboat, he headed back outside, knowing Lou was pissed about him taking his whip. He'd throw a fit if he saw the bubbled paint from the fire. He swung the door open and froze when he felt a gun on the base of his neck.

"Yo, the keys are in my right front pocket. Be easy," Menage said evenly. Lou was gonna be mad.

"Well, well, well, if it ain't Mr. Legend. Turn around!" Scorpion hissed. Menage slowly turned around. "Put your hands on top of your head real slow," he said reaching into Menage's front pocket for the keys. "Do you know who I am, black boy?" Scorpion said in a voice that could easily be mistaken for an actual child's now.

"Don't know and don't care!" Menage said as his adrenaline started to flow.

"Well, I guess I'll just have to see if your daddy, Felix, will pay to keep your ass alive.

What do you think, huh?" Scorpion pushed
the chrome .38 snub nose against Menage's
forehead. Menage involuntarily blinked and
took a step back. "Here," Scorpion said pulling
out a set of cuffs, "put these on . . . and be quick
about it."

Menage took the cuffs and put them on. This
had to be the man who crashed his life, took his
girl and true love, Chandra, killed his unborn
child. Menage's blood began to boil. He wanted
to lash out, but the .38 prevented all of that.

"Holster with no gun, huh? Funny, funny,
funny," Scorpion laughed. Menage didn't
know what the hell he was talking about and
he doubted that anyone would help . . . Black
male, fancy car, held at gunpoint by white
cop, yeah, right!

Scorpion motioned with the .38 for Menage
to go around to the passenger's side of the
Lamborghini. Suddenly out of nowhere, one
of the Blackhawks hovered overhead down
the street as six HRT tactical agents slid
down the two ropes hanging out the door. If
Scorpion were in his right mind, he would have
known that the .38 would cause no real damage
on the Blackhawk at that distance. Even at point
blank range, the Kevlar vests the agents wore
could also have stopped the rounds from doing
them any harm.

Scorpion continued to fire, and Menage didn't think twice about hauling ass back into the warehouse. Throwing down the useless .38, Scorpion jumped into the Lamborghini. There was only one way out, and he hoped speed would pull him out of the jam. Throwing the car in first, he spun it around just as two HRT tactical agents ran from behind a trailer, knelt down tucking their MP5s under their chins and opened up on the fleeing Lamborghini. Scorpion tore down the street, picking up speed as fast as he could. He saw the other four agents from the Blackhawk lined up on the sidewalk, ready to open fire. Leaning to the right as far as he could, he bared his teeth as the fusillade opened up on the Lamborghini. Members of the HRT thought their suspect was out of his mind if he thought the car would make it through the trap. Maybe if he had APC shit, but a thinly covered Lamborghini, not a chance in hell.

Bullets hit the tires, windows, and doors. Scorpion felt the steering wheel jerk beneath his grip, but he never felt the lead tear into his hip as the car flipped over onto its side and then the roof. The audible spit from the MP-5 followed the car as sparks flew from contact with the pavement. Still on its roof, the Lamborghini slid to a stop, chrome wheels spinning.

Scorpion managed to pull himself out of the car and lay on the ground. Out of breath and bleeding, he squinted his eyes from the sun as the six HRT tactical agents stood above him. He could feel his head resting in broken glass and something wet. He closed his eyes and smiled. The CIA would want to know a lot from him, and they knew if they slipped just once he'd escape. When he tried to roll over onto his stomach, a sharp pain shot through his left leg. However, he didn't let on that he was in any pain whatsoever.

"Tell Blue Two to block off the entrance and to not let any one through. I don't care if it's the DCI himself, Walters ordered. He stepped between the six tense HRT tactical agents. Menage stood behind them, eyeing Scorpion as he lay on the ground.

"Eugene, Eugene," Walters said slowly, squatting on the balls of his heels by Scorpion's head. "I finally gotcha. You caused a lot of trouble down here in sunny Miami, caused a high body count too. And the DCI and the powers that be . . . well, they aren't too happy with that, so they sent me to . . . calm you down you can say. You do remember me from Great Britain, right? I knew something was fishy about you botching that hit on our friend at the Embassy, the same one who was going to pay you to kill Felix and then double cross us. Yes, I've done my home-work."

"F-fuck you, S-Stanley," Scorpion stuttered, coughing up blood. "You know the r-rules . . . so g-get me up and take me in."

Walters made a motion with his hand, telling the HRT to hold off. "Yeah, you're right," he said standing.

Menage was still in cuffs as Walters reached for his arm. "Get the fuck off me!" he said jerking backward. "How the hell you gonna let him live!"

Agent Walters held up his hands. "Uh, Mr. Legend, this is way, way over your head, so I think it would be best for you to just walk away. But first let's get those cuffs off." He led Menage a few yards away from the car. As another agent removed the cuffs, Walters took out a butane lighter. Once it was lit, he looked at the orange and blue flame. He thought about how Scorpion would be questioned by the FBI and CIA. It would go on endlessly.

"I need to stop smoking," he said to himself. "Fire in the hole!" he yelled flinging the lighter toward the car. "Everyone hit the ground as the Lamborghini and Scorpion became engulfed in flames. Walters looked at Menage. "I guess it slipped," he said with a broad smile.

Chapter 9

Last Night Stand

*Two Weeks Later Saturday Night
10:48 p.m.*

Menage sat in his living room slumped in his couch, wearing alligator shoes, brown suede baggy pants, a leather and mesh Gucci pullover Jacket, and a brown suede bucket hat. He wore a thick, new platinum chain and spinning medallion that displayed his initials. Vapor lay on the floor by his feet. With his feet propped on the table, head laid back, hat low over his eyes, and hands behind his head, Menage evaluated his life. Benita had dropped by a few days earlier, but he refused to let her into his heart.

"You need to wake up and see that money or what you wear or drive will never bring you true love. Every breath I take is because of you saving my life. But you need to save your own life, Menage, because the world you live in ain't the truth . . . I need you to love me." Those were her last words before she walked out the door. And she had never seen his *Legend* medallion because her cousin had packed it in his suitcase before going back to North Carolina by mistake, supposedly.

No matter how much he tried to deny it, his heart was broken. He hated the fact that he had caught feelings for Benita or anyone else. With over two million to his name, he was still alone. He felt a little guilty about the way he had treated women, but it wasn't like he forced them into his bed, he reasoned. *Fuck it!*

DJ somehow slipped from Felix's so-called plan, and no one knew where he was. The chop shop remained shut down. But paper was still rolling in from the beauty salons, so for now it was all gravy. He heard his Nokia chime, and he knew it was Dough-Low by the tone.

"Yeah," he said reaching down to rub Vapor.

"Yo, 'Nage, you ready?"

"Yeah, what it look like?"

"Parkin'-lot pimpin! They got a car ramp in the VIP limelight parkin' lot for the hottest ride of the night. So far some nigga got the props in a Benz G wagon. But yo, is everything straight?"

"Yeah, just hope it don't go down like Bruce Lee's son!" Menage said nervously.

By voice command, he put the entire mansion in a deep blue setting as a song by Floetry caused a single tear to run down his cheek. Every time a woman got close to him, there was pain. Chandra, Benita, and Lydia . . . Lydia . . . he could still feel her gentle touch, smell the sweet scent of her hair, hear her soft voice, but it all ended in pain.

"Okay, I'ma call ol' boy and tell him to come through 'bout four o'clock. You sure everything straight?" Dough-Low asked again.

"Yeah."

"Oh, it's true!"

Menage ended the call, tossing his phone onto the couch. Standing up, he looked around his empty mansion and knelt down to talk to Vapor. "You my boy, ain't cha? We gon' be all right, boy. Angel Falls is where we're going." Vapor whined and licked his face. Menage stood up straight again. "CD nine, song ten," he said, forcing himself to snap out of it. Seconds later, DMX's "Slippin'" filled the mansion, his thug mansion.

Materialism

Preoccupation with worldly objects comforts and considerations as opposed to spiritual or intelectual values.

Menage trailed his fingers over the hood of his new whip in his garage. The triple-platinum plated rims were custom made and had the same hook-up as he had on his S600, only these rims were 22s resting under a sedan. The color was black with chrome trim on the doors and kit. The glass roof changed colors depending on the sun. Speakers were placed on either side of the interior and two fifteen-inch woofers were behind the back seat. The amps were fitted in a velour and glass case. Menage didn't need a key; the car was unlocked when he placed his thumb on a square on the door and there was another one hidden inside to start the engine.

"My world," he said closing the door. Taking his Gucci shades off the rearview mirror and putting them on, he adjusted the black snake-skin and leather seat. "CD one, song ten, volume max." "So Many Tears" by Tupac shook the whip as the twenty-two-inch rims started spinning and the garage door slowly lifted. Each tinted window began to lower a couple of inches.

Rolling past the gate, he hit the lights and headed to the club. He glanced at the empty passenger's seat. He knew what he had known all along, that money couldn't buy true love. *Maybe Benita was right . . . fuck dat slut!* he thought, his mind going back to her dancing at that party Lou had told him about. All she wanted was money.

Why is it wrong to seek the finer things in life, to be known? Who wants to be average? Different paths should be traveled, and some to the end. Only then can you look back and decide if it was the right path to take or not. And as far as the finer things in life are concerned, the shit on TV ain't no joke; it's like a drug, The iced-out chains, the chick with a twenty-two-inch waist, and a phat ass . . . women won't look twice at a brother working at Burger King or some low-budget gig, No, a nigga gotta be a thug, bust his gun, kill his own kind. Thug love is what they call it. But love ain't real anyway; everybody cheats, so to hell with matters of the heart.

Menage's mind was made up regarding seeking what made him happy, what would keep his heart fully content. Cruising down Twenty-seventh Avenue, he ignored the horns, the chicks waving at him or his whip down . . . off to the Limelight.

"Girl, are you sure Menage said he was coming tonight?" Irish said dressed in a pink, tight-fitting Puma bodysuit and high heels, leaning on the front end of Passion's blue Audi S4.

"Yeah," Passion said, vigorously searching the

parking lot for his Benz, Escalade or Acura. She missed Menage desperately, and she was certain that her outfit would get his attention, a thong, high heels, and skimpy top-all covered by a knee-length fishnet pullover.

Dough-Low sat on the hood of his Yukon Denali XL, smoking a blunt in the VIP section of the Limelight parking lot as the phat test whip contest was still going on. It was down to the G-wagon and a topless white Lexus LS-430 sitting on twenties. Dough-Low looked at his watch. The parking lot was jam-packed. Chicks in Baby Phat skirts and Manolo boots stood in groups, checking out who was balling, fronting or stunting. Niggas were holding digital camcorders, following chicks with phat asses, horns were blowing, and systems booming. As far as Dough-Low was concerned, it was a parking lot freaknik, and proof of that was nearby. Just a few feet away, he noticed a chick in the back of a Lexus LX-470, bouncing up and down as a pair of arms reached up from behind her, squeezing her tits. Two guys waited for their turn while watching the show.

The topless LS-430 was about to be rolled onto the elevated ramp and the judge appeared.

Meanwhile, a large crowd had formed near the entrance of the parking lot. A new whip had come on the scene, and chicks began taking off their heels, running to get a closer look and hoping the passenger's seat was empty.

Menage sat behind the wheel of his game-changing Maybach 62 as a group of girls motioned him forward. He could see the envy in every nigga's eye as he slid the rear windows down to show off the reclined back seats. With Three 6 Mafia banging from the system, the Maybach 62 parted the materialistic crowd like the Red Sea. One girl walked up and mouthed, "You can get it," while pointing to the thick print showing in her boy shorts. All because of his ride, women were stepping to him making promises of sex before they even thought about giving their names.

The show wasn't over. Along with the remote twenty-two inch platinum rims, a bluish glow emitted from under the wheel well to put more focus on the rims. Passion walked through the crowd with her lips pursed and hands resting on her hips. She trailed a finger over the hood as Menage stepped out of his whip. "Putting on a show, huh?" She was afraid he would dis her and take his pick of some other girl that would no doubt drop the panties and get it on in the back of the Maybach. He surprised her by sliding his thumb over the print of her left nipple. "Dis a everyday thang, sexy."

Passion liked Menage's new look, too. He now sported a short haircut with waves and a razor sharp edge-up. Passion felt it couldn't get any better as she walked with him straight into the club, getting VIP status. Menage walked up to the bar, ordered a two-hundred-dollar bottle of Henny, pulled out his Nokia, and called the deejay and requested a song. "Let's twerk it," he said leading her to the mirrored dance floor as a hot beat filled the club. With her back to him and eyes closed, she enjoyed the feel of his hands on her waist. Usually he would have a circle of chicks surrounding him, but tonight it was all about her. And she was quick to put another chick in check if any one of them tried to push up on her man . . . well, her man for tonight, anyway.

Menage was now in his element as a song by Wu Tang rocked the club. Passion swung her hips back and forth as the strobe lights and spinning dance floor created a mind-numbing visual effect. Passion observed Menage's moves, and she could now definitely say that he moved on the dance floor as well as he did in bed. That thought alone made her reach down and playfully grip his ass.

The deejay kept the club moving, and Passion stayed on the floor with Menage because she was determined not to let anybody snatch him up. And it didn't hurt that the music was hot. The steady beats played on as she lost herself in Menage's embrace. Passion observed the thug gazes from the sidelines, fellas showing off their shine, a few throwing up gang signs. She was glad Menage didn't roll with a gang. Her cousin was a Crip, God rest his soul. Grinding his hips against Passion, Menage really did realize that his life was what he made it and that he couldn't save the world. "Put God first," his mother always said. But could he give up the club, the women, the whips, the shine, the drugs? He closed his eyes and brought Passion closer to him. She was real, in his arms, able to take care of his needs. She was now.

"And though my soul was deleted, I couldn't see it." Tupac was right on the money, Menage thought. *Fuck it, my way.* The women started yelling, squealing, and holding up their drinks when the lights went off and switched to red as a hit by Monica filled the club. Menage looked deeply into Passion's eyes as she placed her arms

around his neck. He French kissed her through the entire song and she felt as if her inner thighs would melt. She was grateful when the music changed to some thing fast because she felt herself becoming wet.

After two more songs, they took a break and went back up to VIP. Menage did his best to adjust the small device that poked into his lower back, and the special vest felt too damn tight. Passion watched him glance at his Bulova for the thousandth time, and she asked him what was wrong.

"Nah, it's nothing," he said wishing he could tell the truth.

"So do you want me to come over to your place tonight?" Passion asked sliding her hand back and forth over the erection in his jeans.

He enjoyed her touch for a few seconds before he spoke. "Yeah . . . but if I'm not there, I'll be at Angel Falls."

"Say what?" she asked raising her left eyebrow. "Angel Falls . . . where's that?"

"Never mind, sexy," he said, and kissed her on the lips in the dark VIP booth, sliding his tongue into her mouth. Reaching between her thighs, he cupped her sex just to get her mind off of what he had just said. Passion pulled out his erection and moved her thong to one side. They played with each other until things got beyond hot.

When it neared almost four in the morning, Menage told Passion that he was ready to go. As she went to find Irish, he got up and walked toward the exit. He saw Dough-Low at the bar, looked at his Aqua Swiss Iceberg watch and nodded his head. When he got outside, he pressed his thumb on the sensor of the Maybach. He got in, closed his eyes and placed his forehead on the wheel. "CD four, song two, volume mid." The sounds of Tupac and Biggie filled the lavish vehicle as Menage activated the spinning rims. Letting out a deep breath, he sat back and looked up through the glass roof. "The game will make me or break me," he said to himself. He felt a chill run up his arm as he gripped the wheel and held back the tears that welled up in his eyes. "My world," he whispered.

He got himself together and looked at his watch once more. It was just a couple of minutes before four now. He stepped out of his car and stood in front of the Limelight. "My world," he said again as Wyclef and Mary J. Blige's "911" boomed from his speakers. The club was starting to empty out, and he looked on silently as women began singing along with the song.

"Come on, Irish!" Passion said tugging on her to move through the slow moving crowd. "There Menage go right there!" she said, pointing him out, smiling from ear to ear. The music from the Maybach filled the parking lot.

Menage stood there, noticing all the attention he was getting. He knew he was far from a role model and that it was all based on materialism . . . all based on bullshit. Suddenly, a dark blue Mazda 626 screeched to a stop a few yards from where he stood. It all went down so fast. Irish and Passion could only scream when they realized what was happening, but it was use-less. The first shot went through the crowd, causing several people to scatter and few to go back inside the club. Only two individuals remained, Dough-Low and Passion. Seven shots had gone off quickly and loudly. It seemed, to Passion, that it took forever for the shooting to stop, but by the time the last three shots were fired, Menage was on his knees. Passion saw it all the fine red mist of blood from each hit to his chest and stomach. The Mazda sped off, leaving Menage flat on his face. Passion was the first to reach him, crying and screaming out his name and stomping her feet in place like a small child. Dough-Low ran past her and scooped up Menage, putting his body in his Maybach 62 and peeling out of the parking lot at a high speed before the Ds showed up. Still in a daze and crying, Passion dropped to her knees, declaring her love for Menage Unique Legend.

What could be more pathetic than to be a black man and live and die without ever experiencing the true aspect of loving a black woman?

ORDER FORM
URBAN BOOKS, LLC
97 N. 18th Street
Wyandanch, NY 11798

Name (please print):_____

Address:_____

City/State:_____

Zip:_____

QTY	TITLES	PRICE

Shipping and handling-add $3.50 for 1st book, then $1.75 for each additional book.
Please send a check payable to:
Urban Books, LLC
Please allow 4-6 weeks for delivery